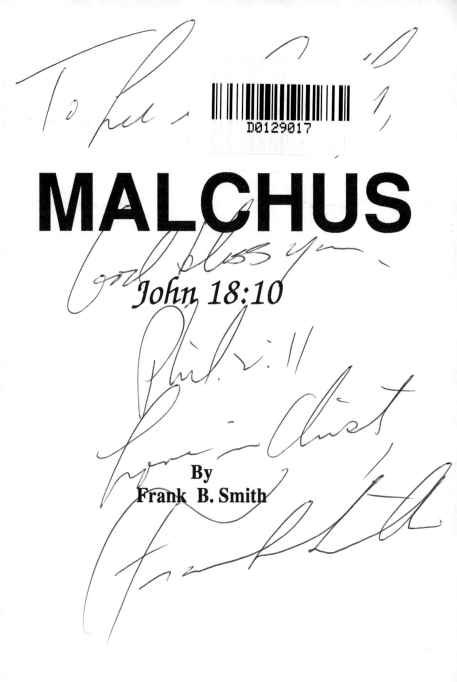

MALCHUS

John 18:10

By
Frank B. Smith

First printing, March 1991

Published by
CRUSHED GRAPES PUBLISHING
P.O. Box 3009 Vista, CA. 92085-3009

Printed in the United States of America
ISBN 0-9618197-2-3

To Derwyn
and the millions
like him.

Books by Frank B. Smith
Ultimate Evangelism, The Church in the Harvest Age.
Conditional Love.
Malchus.

CHAPTER ONE

It's a cold night, yet drops of sweat are running down my sides. I've got to get this done, it must be settled once and for all. I have no choice. I am leading a group of men up a hill to a garden on the Mount of Olives. We have some torches, but since I'm in the front, I run in darkness. It should be just ahead. Come on, come on! I wish we didn't have to rely on that snake Judas. I don't like him. I haven't liked him from the day he came to make a deal with us.

Judas shouts to turn in here. We do, and sure enough, here is the band of scum among a grove of twisted trees. I step on the hand of the first one. The next one is on hands and knees, trying to shake off his slumber and get to his feet. I kick him in the groin, and smile as I hear him groan. The mob moves on past me into a clearing. The leader they call Jesus, and three of his followers are there at the far edge.

As I push my way towards the front, I see Judas walk out from the now stationary troop. Slowly but steadily he crosses the empty space, goes right to Jesus and kisses him. "Uhhh," my disgust escapes, and I spit on the ground. Any fool who associates with such a traitor and even trusts him with their money deserves the things we have in store for him.

There's mob confusion! Jesus asks, "Who do you want?" I fall down. In fact, I fall down again. With rising anger, I shove my way back to the front. My head hurts from too much wine, but I must finish this business.

"We want Jesus of Nazareth," I shout as I raise my club over my head. I pick him out. I'd rather have the whole mess end in a bloody battle here in this garden than the kind of farce that was planned. I almost get to where I can give a good blow.

The torchlight is reflected in a strange swinging arc right next to my head.

Thwump! I hear a strange sound, and though I don't feel pain, I am shocked and I somehow understand that I am wounded. I see flashes of light. I taste blood in my mouth. I feel light-headed. Instinctively I raise my hand to my ear . . . nothing. I don't feel it. No ear. Only a warm sticky goo that must be blood running through my fingers.

"Aaaaaaaaa," I scream, as I sit up, heart pounding, wet with sweat. When I get my bearings and realize I was reliving that night in a dream, I lie back down and think through what happened next. Remembering those events has always helped.

Jesus said to Peter, "Stop it! Put away your sword. The cup my father gave me, shall I not drink it?" Then He reached out and touched my ear.

Just like it happened more than twenty years ago in Jerusalem, even now in this Roman prison, the warmth of his touch washes my mind and heart and the peace of God settles again in my soul.

* * *

My name is Malchus. I am the second son of Benaiah son of Zeturah, servant of the High Priest of Israel. I too was a bond-slave of Caiaphas during the days of the visitation of the Christ, but now that seems so long ago. I am a prisoner in Rome.

Two days from now this city will be the scene of parties and wild extravagances. Caesar will celebrate his birthday, and many people will let their pent-up emotions loose. The streets will fill with crowds and jugglers, singers and musicians. Wine will flow like a river through Rome and many will drop to the ground and spend the night wherever their senses finally drown in the flood.

The rich and powerful will gladly bless Caesar. After all, he's the one letting them live like kings in their own rights. They will look aside when their slaves and servants get a little rowdy, as long as the revelry stays within limits. They will even give them tokens of appreciation and share with them a tiny portion of their opulent wealth.

The huge mass of slaves and servants will shout and chant, but the unrest and hatred within will not spill out. They have learned well—there is no resistance against Rome. Rome is supreme. Rome conquers all. Rome is invincible. When the Roman legions conquered their lands and took them as slaves to serve in this great city, all options disappeared. They lived, ate, slept, labored, and breathed, only by the mercy of Rome.

Then come the soldiers. Thousands of them, and thousands more who once were soldiers, but are now too old or too crippled to march out to battle. Many of the officers have become wealthy. Others bought positions of status with their share of the plunder. But all of them seem to have glazed eyes looking at something far away. Some hide their memories in huge bowls of wine, while others mask their past with the religion of Rome's destiny and the rightness of their rule. Killing, murder and slavery are justified by this great society. Neither the drinkers nor pretenders will tolerate deviation from Roman domination.

One of these soldiers is Cleomus. He is still on duty, but "limited" as a guard in Rome's infamous prison system. He's probably about my age, but looks much older than I in spite of my white-streaked beard. Battles and hardships have taken their toll. A severely wounded, yet not dead left arm, debilitates and hurts him. There is still enough life in the arm for pain, but not enough to hold a shield. Cleomus' right arm, always strong and powerful, has become massive.

Cleomus compensates for this disability with a pain in- spired fierceness and loyalty to Rome or loyalty to whatever he thinks is good for Rome. Good for Rome usually means what's good for Cleomus. Maybe "good" isn't the best word, because it's more like whatever gives vent to his smoldering rage or relieves his pained edginess. His wincing scowl has etched deep furrows on his face.

Cleomus is in charge of the night watch. He is responsible for four or five other guards. He answers to the centurion who oversees this prison for "political" prisoners, as well as the

7

other prison which handles the crime perpetrators. It is, as typical of Rome, a very efficient operation.

My part in Caesar's birthday party is not yet determined. I have some choice in it. I can swear allegiance to Caesar, and say, "Caesar is Lord!" Or I can be burned like a candle on Caesar's birthday cake; or I may be torn apart by wild animals in the Arena as part of the entertainment for the party; or I may be a decoration lining one of the streets of Rome as I hang from a cross. Oh, dear God, may it not be the cross. Please, may it not be the cross.

I don't want to be morbid—but under the circumstances, I am anyway. Maybe I'm bound to be morbid, but let me tell you about different days. I was going to say happier days but some were and some weren't.

JERUSALEM

My earliest memories are of the noise and confusion in the Temple in Jerusalem. My father isn't part of my first memories. I think I blanked him out of those early times because he was gone so much. When he was around, I was frightened by him.

I remember being in the Court of the Women clutching my mother's leg. There was noise, smoke, strong smells, and crowds pushing and shoving. She spoke harshly to me, "Ouch, Malchus, you're hurting my leg! Stop it!" I cried. I cried because I was terrified by the surroundings and because Mama spoke so harshly.

She lifted me up and began to soothe me. She tried to point out the things that were happening. As I looked through the Court of Israel where the men were, and to the place where all the smoke and smell came from, I couldn't see very well. I didn't want to see either.

I was soon comforted in my mother's bosom. I loved the feel of her breasts and the warm security there. Everything was fine when I nestled at this source of milk, tenderness and love. For my first three years, her breasts were my source of life.

Later on, I remember being jealous of my younger brothers and sisters when they nursed at her breasts, but I had to join my older brother and just watch. Sometimes, when we could get away with it, we put a hand on the exposed skin near where brother or sister was nursing. Usually Mama understood and just smiled at us and shifted away. Sometimes though, especially the older I got, she would say, "Stop that, Malchus." I think those words stung harsher than the rod my father used on us.

Father was proud. He walked among the people with an air that said, "I'm important. Keep your distance." He walked among us the same way.

He took the rod to us when he had to, but there were many times we deserved it and did not get it. I felt he did it because the law said to. It was like he did it to please those people who knew he did it. As far as we were concerned he didn't care one way or the other, so long as we didn't embarrass him.

I never liked going to the Temple, and that first fear and discomfort never left me. Whenever we joined the crowds, I started to panic. I didn't break away as I wanted to, because I was afraid of the rod. This was Father's big show, and I was certain to get the rod if I ran back home.

Once when I was five or six, I bolted from my mother's side and ran home. I was sitting by our wall scratching figures in the dirt. "See, I can do what I want. I can be anything. I can come home when I want. I can make all these dirt people, and be happy. I don't have to go to that terrible place."

Then Father came up the path. He was walking fast. His face was red. He grabbed me. My arm hurt and I tried to pull away. He gripped me like a vise. He dragged me back towards the terrible place. I kicked and screamed, "No! No! I won't go!. I hate it!"

Father said nothing, but when we came to a tree he broke off a branch and beat me. It wasn't like any other time. He hit me and hit me and hit me. He stopped because he saw the people around and some of the women had started to stare. Then he pinched my ear, and with my ear leading the way, he dragged me back to Mama's side. All he said to her was, "Here."

Father never mentioned this again, but often, in the night, I suffered the same beating in my mind. In my dream I was again in that terrible place with the screaming animals and just as I was about to escape, my father would appear and pull me by the ear all the way to the altar. I would be drowning in a sea of blood and one of the priests would come towards me with a sharp knife—at that point I usually woke up screaming in a cold sweat.

Sometimes Mama came and comforted me in the night. As I grew older she didn't come as much. When I got close to manhood she didn't come at all. I would lie hot and sweaty on my mat, wide awake. I tried to stay awake, but often sank into a deep sleep with no covers over me. On those mornings, I awoke chilled and sick.

As I approached the age of twelve, I began to feel uncomfortable. I was to become a man, "gadol," a big one, but I really wanted to stay with the younger "katons." Father took more of an interest in me. He said, "Malchus, soon I will take you into the Court of Israel and because we are Levites, and I am servant to the High Priest, I will even take you into the Court of the Priests." I did not dare answer, and my father put his own interpretation on my wide-eyed, tongue-tied responses.

Well, the day arrived in spite of all my apprehensions. Just before dawn, father shook me from sleep, "Wake up Malchus, get up." We walked the short distance from our home to the Temple, in pitch darkness. We knew the way well. Lights were gleaming from the Court of Israel and the court of the Priests where the duty priests were already casting lots for the day's ministry.

The Temple, the terrible place, was even more foreboding in the dark. No crowds, no noise. The animals weren't even awake when we walked through the huge Court of the Gentiles. Then we entered the Sacred Enclosure and The Court of the Women. That's where I wanted to stay, but not one person was there. As we walked quickly through the empty Court of the Women Father said: "You will leave this place and no longer be welcome here with the women and children." It wasn't as if I was going on to something else, but my safe refuge was being taken away. Father put his hand on my shoulder, something I don't remember happening on any other day of my life. It felt like it would push me through the floor. I stumbled and he removed it for awhile. I was glad it was gone.

Even the Court of Israel had only a few worshippers, but more were coming as the time drew near for the morning sacrifice. We hurried on into the very Court of the Priests. Although we were Levites and thus part of the priestly tribe, we were not priests and should not have been there. I thought, "Maybe God will strike me dead and get me out of this place." No such luck.

Everyone knew Father. "Shalom Eliechim, Benaiah. Who is this man with you?"

I suppose they all meant well, but I wanted to yell, "No! I'm not a man. I am Malchus, and I belong back there in the Court of the Women with Mama and the children, not here with you cruel butchers."

I was glad we didn't have time to eat because my stomach was doing strange things and the emptiness was a relief. Things were happening and I didn't want to be conspicuous.

The gray of dawn began to show and things really started happening. A lamb was led out of the lamb house, and a parade of priests carried all their tools and utensils to the Great Altar.

The Great Altar was huge, and the fire that always burned had just been rekindled. Father said the priests who were on duty that week were from somewhere up north, and they had already cast lots to see who got to do the different things. The first lot was to attend the fire, and the second was to see who got to kill the lamb.

The staggering, just awakened lamb was led to the Altar. A beautiful golden bowl was used to give it a last drink of water. Then its legs were tied. I identified with the lamb feeling like I was tied up.

I was startled by the loud blast of a trumpet. I'd heard the trumpet before, but never from so close. It scared me. My heart raced, which helped me survive the murdering of the lamb. Suddenly, I was enraged. When they cut it open and threw the blood on the altar I didn't get sick.

The huge, beautiful doors to the Holy Place opened and I felt awe. I could clearly see the big gold vine over the doors and the man-sized clusters of grapes. I knew what was inside. I felt like God was involved with the things going on inside more than with all the bloody stuff out where we were.

More priests went in and trimmed the lamps. I tried to concentrate on what was happening inside because I knew they were hacking the dead lamb and I didn't want to see it. Then several hundred priests in their robes and turbans came together and drew lots again. This time the one in charge said a prayer and in unison they all said the Shema. "Hear, O Israel, the Lord, our God, is one Lord." Goose-bumps covered my arms.

One old priest started dancing and shouting. Father said he drew the lot to burn incense, and so will be called rich and holy. He'll never get to draw the lot for that again no matter how long he lives or how many times his priestly group serves in the Temple. My interest continued to rise.

They chose another priest for something and then most of them left. Father said they went to their rooms to change clothes and do whatever they wanted. Amidst all the activity, I saw the musicians and singers getting into their places. Behind us, in the Court of Israel, the stationary men took their places as representatives of the people for the morning sacrifice.

The old priest and two others went into the Holy Place. One carried live coals from the Great Altar, and the other incense, then they left. A hushed silence spread throughout the Temple. I watched a cloud of smoke rise from within the Holy Place. Soon the old priest came out, too. He lifted his arms and blessed us. I was shocked to hear the name of God actually spoken, but . . . more shocks soon followed.

As the musicians and singers began, my father's heavy hand was back on my shoulder and he guided me closer to the Great Altar. The smoke and odors exploded all around me. Another priest was putting the butchered lamb on the altar, and then he lifted a handful of innards to show us. I saw the bright yellow fat that covered the kidneys, some organs and intestines in and falling out of his hand, and the blood of the innocent victim running down the priest's forearm. I started retching.

My head was spinning. I almost passed out and fell into the sea of blood at my feet. When I realized I was standing in blood, I threw up.

Later at home after I was cleaned up, Father told me that many people get sick. I appreciated his attempt to be kind, but I knew he was embarrassed. From then on, he seemed to avoid me. He would have to wait for another son to rejoice in his bloody, cruel world.

CHAPTER TWO

Cleomus sees that I am awake and covered with sweat. He heard me shout in my sleep a little while ago, but outbursts are common in this prison. He comes into my cell and gruffly demands, "What's the matter, Malchus?"

"Nightmare. I had a nightmare."

"What happened?"

"Oh I was just reliving something that happened about twenty years ago."

"Tell me about it. I'm bored, entertain me. What was it?"

"You probably don't want to hear about it, Cleomus. It's about Jesus, and when I was a part of the ones who killed him."

"You were one of the people that killed him?"

"I had intended to be, but when we arrested him something happened that changed all that. I started a seven week journey through hell and back that has wound up here twenty years later."

"So, what happened?"

"I was a bond-slave of Caiaphas the High . . ."

"You were a slave?"

"No, not really a slave, but yes, I was. A bond-slave is someone who agrees to serve a person for life just like a slave. It's like you soldiers. You're sort of like slaves to Rome, yet you've got some choice in it. You know what I mean?"

"Yeah, yeah, what happened?"

"Well, Caiaphas and the other elders of the Jews figured Jesus had to go. He was a threat to them. They worked out a deal with a traitor named Judas. We were to go and arrest him in the middle of the night when the crowds weren't around. They were worried about the people and what they might think."

14

"I was leading a group of soldiers from the temple. We were armed to the teeth against this Jesus and twelve or so of his followers. We didn't expect any resistance, but when we got there, one of his disciples named Peter hit me with a sword and cut off my ear."

Cleomus leans down and scowls hard at my ears. "You got ears. What do you mean, he cut off your ear?"

"He cut it off alright, but then Jesus touched me and healed it. He put it back."

"That's ram's dung." Cleomus grabs my tunic with his one good arm and jerks me up to my feet. His face is in my face. Boiling mad he continues, "You stinking Christians expect me to believe all this ram's dung you keep piling on me. You must think I'm crazy! You must think we're all crazy! Rose from the dead! Put back a cut-off ear!"

He slams me back on my mat with a frightening viciousness that strangely, I do not feel. As he stalks off, I say to myself, "Well, he listened longer than ever before. And, he really didn't hurt me."

I think Cleomus started changing about a month ago. Our prayers for him are being heard. I understand how he feels. I'd felt that way too! I hated Christians. I had even hated my own wife for awhile. Oh, how I long for her now.

Oh Lord, please bless Bethany. Watch over her and keep her strong in You." How I wish she were here—not in this prison, but here where I could talk with her, and hold her. I think I'm wishing I could be there with her.

JERUSALEM

Bethany was the daughter of my mother's uncle, a silver-haired priest named Asaph. She grew up in Galilee, about a three days' journey north of us. I saw her at least once a year, but often several times.

Since her father was a priest, he religiously followed the law. During the feasts of Passover and Weeks, and again for

Tabernacles, he would come to Jerusalem. He would also come whenever his priestly course was on duty at the Temple.

Often he would bring his family with him, and they usually stayed at our house. During Tabernacles, when we lived in booths, our whole visiting family set up these shelters in our yard. We were wealthy and had a huge yard, so relatives from all over the country came and stayed at our place.

What a time we had! The meals were incredible. Some of our relatives were good cooks, and the rest of them were excellent. We shared the meals together and served ourselves from a common table with platters of delicious dishes piled high. At each meal an aunt or a cousin, or even several of them, would accost me with: "What's the matter, Malchus? Don't you like my cooking? Here child, eat! How do you ever expect to grow?"

Eat I did, we all did. We ate until we could hardly leave the tables, but before long we would all be playing some kind of game. We would run around and hide and laugh, and tease the younger children and mimic the older ones. Those times at the festivals, especially Tabernacles, are the best memories of my early life.

Even as children we understood that Tabernacles meant God Himself would come and share life with us. He would "tabernacle" with us, and we celebrated with a great party. Although I hated the bloody sacrifice business, I loved a God who would come and tabernacle with us.

We also sang and prayed as a family, but not long, boring prayers. The singing wasn't boring either. We sang the Psalms of David. Some were a little slow, but lots of them were lively and fun to sing.

And dance, did we ever dance! All of us danced. Adults, children, parents, grandparents. All of us. Only those who were too old would sit out, but before long dancers began to drop out and join those clapping and cheering us on. We danced until we dropped from exhaustion.

In the evening we would all sit around a big fire. The oldest man would tell about the Exodus from Egypt, and how our fathers lived in tents for forty years. They also told stories about

Moses, and Samuel, and Gideon, and how our fathers defeated the Philistines, and the mighty exploits of King David.

Then we'd laugh and laugh when they sprinkled in stories like how Uncle Jeniah got locked in a toilet house when he was about eight years old, and was stuck there for three hours. Or how grandmother set a trap for Zeturah because she thought he was such a good catch. He was doing the same for her, and they met each other right in the middle of their schemes.

I was a part. We were a family, and we were part of the people of God. Those were the days!

I had always liked Bethany, but had avoided her simply because she was a girl. But when I was sixteen, just before she turned sixteen, I noticed her like I'd never noticed anyone before, or after.

It happened just about sunset, when I was gathering wood for the evening fire. We had all been praying after the evening meal. Bethany was obviously touched by the love of God, for she was still worshipping. Her arms were raised unto the Lord. Her face was slightly tilted back with an incredible expression of trust, love and gratitude. It was a very holy moment with a devotion meant for God alone, yet I was there.

I felt like an intruder, but I was held to this vision by the setting sun directly behind her. It illumined her through her clothes as if she were standing there with only a filmy lace covering her beautiful body. Her breasts were formed with a perfection of beauty. These were not just future milk suppliers for infants. Solomon must have seen something like this when he said, "Let her breasts satisfy you always."

I then saw her hips and the incredible curviness of her body. I was entranced. I kept hearing something, but it was like a pesky fly buzzing around my ear. It was my name being spoken over and over. I came out of the trance when Uncle Asaph took hold of my arm.

"Malchus, what's wrong with you?" As he followed my gaze and saw the vision of his own daughter he said, "Oh, that's what it is."

He led me by the arm to the fire area and began helping me with the wood I was carrying. He said: "David was right, wasn't he, when he said, 'I am fearfully and wonderfully made'?"

After a few moments of silence he asked, "Well, isn't it so Malchus?"

"Yes sir," stumbled out of my mouth.

"Is your heart set on her?"

Again, "Yes sir." I had not thought of her in this way before, but I would never think of her in any other way from then on.

* * *

My father Benaiah was the servant of Annas, who was the High Priest for nine years, up until I was about twelve. His son Eleazar followed him for two years, but his son-in-law, Joseph Caiaphas, took over when I was fourteen, and ruled for eighteen years as the High Priest of Israel.

Old Annas was shrewd. He knew when to cozy up to the Romans, and when to do what he wanted. He was a Sadducee and his beliefs were second to his politics. Not his political beliefs, but his lust and craving for meddling in politics. He didn't care so much what happened, as long as it happened at his direction.

He treated his sons well as they grew up, and consequently they did not have his intensity and lust for power. His son-in-law Caiaphas, however, was perfectly suited to follow in his footsteps.

When he reached his mid-fifties, Annas stepped down from the High Priesthood, but he never budged a centimeter from his position power over the Sanhedrin. The Sanhedrin was the council of seventy, the ruling body of the Israelites. It was made up of Sadducees and Pharisees, or liberals and conservatives, or politicians and religionists. It took a kind of genius to keep this body functioning.

Although we were under Roman rule in Judea, the Roman administrator stayed in Caesarea. He came to Jerusalem only for important days, or if there was trouble, and he let us Jews run our own affairs so long as we kept the Pax Romana and paid our taxes.

Father would not talk about how he came into the service of Annas. I suspected there was something shady in it. Annas trusted father, and the ring in father's ear was a mark of lifelong servitude to Annas. We were wealthy and very influential. Father would sit in at all the meetings of the Sanhedrin, unless Annas sent him on an assignment. He was always at Annas' disposal.

* * *

It was taken for granted that my brothers and I would become merchants, or dignitaries, or rabbis, or something of importance in our society. It was also necessary for us to be apprenticed in a trade.

Father encouraged me to consider being trained as a cobbler. Old Ziph just two streets down towards Kidron had always made our sandals and was willing to train me for a four year period. "What do you think, Malchus?"

It was, of course, father's decision, but it seemed important to him that I concurred. "Yes, sir. It sounds good to me."

From the vantage point of the years, I can see that my ordeal with Ziph was good for me. But for a time it was horrible. Much later I realized that father probably asked him to be tough on me to harden me up for life. Ziph took the assignment with eagerness.

"So, the little rich kid wants to be a cobbler?" he sneered just after father left me in his care. "We'll see what kind of stuff you're made of. You'll probably go whining home to momma to get you out of it, won't you?"

Ziph would ask me sarcastic questions and if I fell into the trap and answered them, he used the answers as barbs to prod over and over again. Maybe I was a rich kid, but I wasn't dumb. I soon learned not to answer these questions, and also not to complain at home.

Mother was sympathetic, and my early complaining caused her a lot of grief. I loved her too much to wish upon her the burden of my misfortune. At thirteen years old I was a man, and I learned to carry it myself. Besides, there was nothing Mother could do for me.

"Oh, little rich kid's got soft hands? Poor boy. Maybe you can pay somebody to work the needle for you? Huh Malchus?"

My hands were raw. The rough leather and the punch and the needle combined to chew up my flesh. Ziph could have given me some other things to do at first, while my hands and fingers got tough, but he would not pass up a chance to make me suffer.

First my thumb began to bleed, then my index finger, then the side of my index finger on my left hand. The skin on my thumb pad began to perforate. I didn't have to wonder if Ziph knew about it because he yelled at me, "Don't get blood on the leather. It stains and it's hard to get out."

"Filthy scum," I thought.

When I went home, I could not eat with my hands. I wasn't hungry anyway, and mother poured oil and wine on the wounds and wrapped them with clean cloths. Bethany should see me now. Mother's tenderness and concern were a comfort, but that night was fitful and I dreamed of the poor, dead, bloody lamb being hacked to pieces on the Great Altar.

The second day was worse than the first. I could not use my hands at all, so Ziph said, "So the poor little rich boy couldn't do the work? What's the matter Malchus, can't take the pressure? Maybe you should apprentice to be a midwife. Ha ha ha ha," came the sarcastic laughter.

"Well since you're too puny to be any good here, go to the tanner and get my skins."

It was a warm day with little or no wind. I followed carefully the directions Ziph gave me, but was beginning to think I had missed a turn or taken a wrong path. I had left the city more than an hour before, and was walking fast. I had taken the road south toward Bethlehem. After passing Herod's Pools, I turned right along what began as a well worn path.

A sickening stench began to hang in the air. I saw some buildings ahead which I assumed were the tanner's place, since nothing else was anywhere around. I thought there must be a dead animal here near the path, and I would soon get away from the choking smell. It got worse and worse. The closer I came to the tanner's, the stronger the aroma.

The stench was so offensive that I thought I heard it as well as smelled it—like a whirring, spinning, grinding that heightened the smelling. Besides this, I could feel the nausea sweeping in waves through my body.

"Well wool-faced, shaky one, you must be old Ziph's new apprentice. Welcome. Welcome to my lonely house and shop. Come in. Sit down. Would you like some refreshment? I have some delicious cool buttermilk."

I could not talk. I clenched my mouth shut hard.

"Oh yes, forgive me. I forget what it is like the first time you come so close to us lonely ones. Well, you get over it. Let me see your hands."

He looked at my hands, now swollen and pink. He frowned and said, "I have something to help you." And then before I could protest, he put on an ointment that hardened quickly. It felt soothing. I couldn't tell then because it smelled so strong everywhere, but the stuff he put on my wounded hands carried the odor for several days. I was glad Bethany wasn't around then.

I liked Bartholomew the tanner, and over the years of apprenticeship I began to look forward to these trips. During the second visit I was even able to eat with him. I made the trip once or twice a month.

My hands eventually healed and became as tough as the leather they worked. I even avoided the use of the leather shield the cobblers wore when using the needle. It was a matter of pride to me. Since Ziph had denied me its use that first day, I would not use it from then on.

I hated Ziph. I knew no other reaction than hatred to his cruel behavior and malicious teasing. After a few months, however, I noticed that the hatred was not there. I accepted Ziph for the miserable old scoundrel he was.

He hated the rich. That's understandable. Lots of people hate the rich. They're envious. I learned that lesson at an early age. Ziph can keep his bitterness, and I'll keep the money. And, I'll also become the best sandal maker in Jerusalem. I'll show old Ziph that I can be better than he is.

When I came to the shop in the early mornings, he greeted me with some kind of cutting remark. Once my hatred left, I noticed I liked the attention. Even though the remarks were pointed, there was no poison on the barbs. He was what he was, and we had some things in common.

I think he began to enjoy me after a few months. I became pretty good at the work rather quickly. I made his job a lot easier, and he knew it, even if he didn't say anything. After about a year and a half I got quite good, and we began to compete with one another.

We never called it a competition, or ever admitted I had become that good, but we competed hard. If we started a pair of sandals about the same time, we got faster and faster by the finish, racing finger poking speed until one of us finished. If I finished first I would whistle and strut while he grumped around. He could never acknowledge that I beat him.

Of course when he finished first, he rubbed it in. "Stupid rich kids have no business making sandals. I could teach you everything, and you still wouldn't be able to do it right or to keep up." He loved it.

When he died, I went numb. I had finished about three and a half years of the four year apprenticeship when one morning I arrived and Ziph was not in the shop. That had never happened. I called out, "Ziph."

Ziph's wife came into the shop through a door that connected the house with the shop. I don't recall her ever coming into the shop like that. "Ziph's dead. He died in the night." That was all she said. She turned around and went back into the house.

I stood in the empty shop a long time. "Where's my greeting? Who's going to race me? What happens now?"

I walked home and just sat. After a few hours I realized I wanted to pay respects and go to the burial, but when I came to the house, a neighbor said they had already gone and it was too late.

Father arranged with another cobbler to finish my apprenticeship. He probably would have certified me right away, but I finished the six months at his shop. It was not the same. I was more like a hired worker. I missed Ziph and the relationship. I missed him, but by then my mind was so filled with Bethany that I quickly got over the gnawing emptiness inside.

CHAPTER THREE

ROME

It's been half an hour since Cleomus stalked off. I notice him heading back towards my cell. Our prayers are being answered. Surely Cleomus is the most prayed for soldier in all of Rome.

He treated Christians with contempt and hatred. He thought we were crazy, or somehow under a spell. He made life especially miserable for the new ones. They were a convenient outlet for all his pent-up wrath, his pain and anger, and his curious loyalty to Caesar.

About two months ago, a particularly zealous Christian named Demetrius was brought here. Like all new prisoners, he was put into a large common cell. These "pots" as they are called, are dangerous places, where new prisoners quickly learn which other prisoners are trouble, how to avoid the attention of the guards, and what the rules of the house are. You stay in this pot as long as some unknown authority decrees, probably until you realize you are nothing to the jailers and they can do to you whatever they want. The system saves the Romans a lot of time and effort.

I think it was Peter or one of the other apostles who said: "Some new Christians are so zealous, they need to be locked up for six months." It wouldn't have made any difference with Demetrius. He was that zealous.

Demetrius was continually telling other prisoners, "Jesus loves you." Or, "Jesus is alive and would like to enter into a living relationship with you." Or, "Come on, face it. You've made a mess of your life. Jesus can wash and forgive you, and

24

give you a new life that never ends." Sometimes he even said these things to the guards.

Naturally there were responses such as, "Sure, follow your crazy Jewish Rabbi and wind up here like you! That's not much of a life." Sometimes the responses were harsher, and always vulgar.

Cleomus was in an especially foul mood when Demetrius was here only two days. Demetrius was also troubled, but being a single minded new Christian, he thought he would overcome his own problems by being more aggressive. He told Cleomus, "God commands you to repent and change your ways. You must turn from your stinking ways to His ways."

Cleomus roared, "Silence you filthy scum!"

From years of sharp tongued response, Demetrius shot back with, "Look you Roman dirt, you . . ." And then he realized what he had done.

He was in the process of apologizing. He was genuinely sorry for railing like that and said, "I'm sorry Cleomus. I didn't really mean that. I'm just . . ."

Cleomus tore open the door to the common cell, and in spite of his age and wine-enlarged stomach, walked quickly and determinedly towards him. As Demetrius tried to apologize, Cleomus drew his sword and with one powerful swing cut through his neck. His sword was dull from several years of non-combat, but there was enough force to nearly sever Demetrius's entire head. His head flopped and hung from his shoulder as Demetrius's body crumpled to the floor.

Stunned silence hung in the air. Cleomus bent down, wiped his sword on Demetrius' clothes, stood, and without a word walked out. A few minutes later another guard and some slaves came into the cell and carried the body out.

The grieving process was different in prison. We were all facing death or denial, so after a very short time of mourning, we, who were followers of the Way, all concluded that Demetrius died in a most magnificent way. He was following the command of Jesus, though not as gently as we might have liked. He sinned in his sharp response, but he died in the very act of asking forgiveness from the one with whom he was sharing Jesus.

This killing resulted in increased prayer for Cleomus. We prayed for him all the time. I thought that at the judgment day, Cleomus would stand before the Lord Jesus and Demetrius would be at Jesus' side. That vision moved me to pray more for Cleomus than I had for any other non-believer.

Priorities are obvious in a prison like this. Jesus' words to pray for your enemies became clear. We used to ask, "Who is my enemy?" There isn't any question about that here. We are under command to do good to Cleomus, to pray for Cleomus, to forgive Cleomus.

Now, as Cleomus returns after his tirade against Christians that ended with slamming me back on my mat, I am reminded of old Ziph. I smile as he enters my cell.

Cleomus gruffly demands, "Lemme see your ears Malchus."

I offer my head as he scrutinizes one ear, then the other. "There aren't even any scars. What do you take me for, Malchus? Do you think I'd really believe that?"

"When Jesus touched me, Cleomus, he healed me. He put it back as good as it was before."

I got the impression Cleomus wanted to believe me. "How do you know it was cut off?" he asks. "Maybe it was just bruised and all he did was touch you. You know, there really isn't any way to be sure about it."

"I'll tell you why I'm so sure," I say. "When I was just eighteen I wanted to marry Bethany. That was awfully young. I'd finished my apprenticeship, but my father wasn't ready to bless the marriage until I was more settled in work. And work to Father didn't mean being a cobbler. He thought I should be a man of status and rank."

"That's when I became a bond-slave to Caiaphas," I continue. "He was the son-in-law of the most powerful Jew in Judea, a man named Annas. Anyway, Caiaphas needed a servant to do whatever he told him. Not the sort of servant who would clean up his house, but a person he could send to Rome, or Caesarea, and know that the servant would be loyal to him."

"We have a custom, actually a law, about becoming bond-slaves. It was originally for real slaves, who were offered their freedom and chose to stay with the old master because of a wife, family, or for whatever reason. It was in a formal public ceremony that I became the servant of Caiaphas for the rest of my life. I pledged to put his interests above mine; to obey him in everything unless it violated my conscience, and even then, I vowed to tell him why I would not do it."

"That's stupid," Cleomus says. "but your ear. What about your ear. How do you know your ear was cut off?"

"When I became a bond-slave to Caiaphas, there was a ceremony. My father and mother and some other witnesses were there in front of his house. They asked me questions about serving Caiaphas, and heard my vows. Then Caiaphas took an awl and went to the front door of his house and punched a hole in my ear lobe, driving the awl through my ear, into the door frame. It hurt, but it wasn't nearly as bad as I thought it would be. Then they put a gold ring in my ear as a mark that I was a bond-slave."

Cleomus breaks in, "There's no hole or ring in your ear."

"That's just it Cleomus, when Jesus touched my ear and put it back on, the ring was gone."

"Huh," Cleomus grunts, "I'll think about it." He slowly walked away, his eyes fixed on the floor.

In these quiet times of waiting for whatever, I try to pray, try to remember the scriptures I know, try to do anything, yet my mind is like a troop of marching soldiers on a road to examine the times and eras of my life.

I feel detached from my earlier life—as if it were someone else that had been living it. Yet it was me. I am different now, but all those things are a part of what I have now become. I often thought or prayed, "Oh God, are you going to take all that You have made me, and just sacrifice it on a Roman cross? What good would that be? What purpose would that serve?"

JERUSALEM

Bethany filled my mind and heart from the day I saw her, at age sixteen. I counted the days between uncle Asaph's visits to Jerusalem, and I prayed hard that he would bring his family.

When they came, I was ecstatic, but my ecstasy would be short lived when I saw her. Why did my tongue feel so thick? Why did the sores on my face flare up just before they came? Why was I suddenly so clumsy? I wanted so much to impress her, but when she came, I dropped things, stumbled and told her things that were so wonderful while in my mind but sounded so stupid when they came out of my mouth.

Bethany saw me differently. She seemed not to notice my bumbling, or else she was so concerned with the way I saw her, that my shortcomings didn't count. It soon became clear that she was also interested in me.

In my seventeenth year I spent the family times with her. My brothers and cousins would press me to join in the games and adventures, but I said no.

When they realized where my attentions were directed, they teased me. They chanted in childish sing-song, "Malchus loves Bethany." I wanted to be angry, but it was the truth, so I just laughed. Bethany heard them and it seemed to please her. Her face would flush with a crimson coloring she couldn't hide. I loved it.

We would sit together at meals, and evening gatherings. I wanted desperately to hold her, but of course I didn't. Being that close to her, I became aware of her deep love for God. When she told me her highest goal in life was to serve God by being a good wife and mother, I silently prayed, "Oh Lord God, let me be him."

After the Feast of Tabernacles that year, I went to Father and told him of my desire for Bethany. He said that Asaph had talked to him also, and that he would bless the marriage if I had gainful employment. Then he related that Caiaphas would be willing to put me to work, but only if I had my ear punched and became his bond-servant.

It all seemed so matter of fact to Father, but I was so happy with the prospects that I made up for any lack of emotion from him. I knew what being a bond-slave meant, and would have resisted it under other circumstances. But Bethany was worth it. We proceeded with the plans Father and Asaph had worked out.

I turned eighteen that winter. When Asaph brought his family for Passover, Bethany and I were betrothed, or promised to one another. The wedding was not to take place until I had been placed in service to Caiaphas, but the way the families began planning and carrying on, you'd think it was going to happen the next week.

Caiaphas scheduled my ear-piercing for the week after Pentecost, and it seemed good to all that the wedding would take place in Jerusalem just before Tabernacles. That way the families would all be together and I would not have to go to Galilee to take her.

I thought Bethany's family had rented a house near ours for the wedding, but at the giving of gifts following the ceremony the house was given to us as a wedding gift. I went to her father's house to get her, and when we were wed, I took her back to the same house. Our house.

The procession to her house was lengthy. All of her maidens were family and all were happy and excited. Bethany was radiant. I looked into her beautiful eyes and told her, "Bethany, you are the most magnificent thing that God has ever created." The attendants laughed at such a public display, but they were pleased. I took her to my father's house where the canopy had been placed and tables set with abundance of food and gifts.

Asaph always appeared dignified with his silver hair and priestly dress, but he glowed that day like an angel of God. He began the ceremony by questioning me. Did I fear God? Did I love his daughter? Would I care for her and respect her? Would I be faithful to her, and give her the honor she was due?

Asaph obviously cared greatly for Bethany and wanted me to understand the treasure I was receiving and to pledge my loyalty in a way that satisfied him. He then put her hand in mine and said, "I give my daughter to you in the fear of God. You are now responsible for her. Cherish her, Malchus, and raise a godly family. May she be to you as Rachel and Leah, a fruitful vine in your house, and may your sons be like olive plants around your table." It was not proper, but the guests began to cheer.

Father then spoke to us about tradition, and what was right. His words did not carry the life that Asaph's did. The people still cheered, but in a more subdued way.

When we were under the canopy, it was Annas himself that honored us by pronouncing the blessing. During the dancing and celebrating that followed, many said they had never seen such a wedding ceremony. We were truly blessed. I felt that God was favoring our marriage already.

* * *

When we were finally alone, Bethany said, "It was a wonderful ceremony my lord. I am very pleased to be your wife."

I was startled to hear her call me, "my lord." I liked it in a way, but it was very unnerving. "Bethany," I said, "you've called me Malchus for years. Why change that now?"

"But this is all so different now my husband. We were children together, brother and sister almost. Now it is different. You are like Abraham to me, my husband. As Sarah called him lord, so I look to you as my lord, my provider,"

"And as your friend," I interrupted. "We have been friends for a long time Bethany. I am beside myself with the expectations of making love, and I don't know if we are to be Malchus and Bethany, or husband and wife, or lord and servant, or what."

Bethany said tenderly, "We will find out, my lord Malchus."

JERUSALEM

Bethany was all that any man could hope for. She was loyal, loving, and tender. Although we had our times of disagreements, she was quick to apologize if she felt she was wrong. For about five years we experienced happiness and fulfillment that brought balance to my life as the servant of Caiaphas.

With Caiaphas I was like a different person.

At first he wanted me to just be with him. He would ask me to do little stupid things. At times I thought I was in for a horribly boring life running little errands for Caiaphas. I was ambitious. I wanted to do. I wanted to be. And, since it was my place in life to serve this man, I wanted to make him the greatest man on the earth. I wanted to prove the sincerity of my vows.

After a few months he asked me to take care of a rather touchy situation. There was a widow, well off financially, whose husband had dedicated their home to God. It was declared "Corban." Now it seemed the widow was staying in the house, and the matter needed to be settled.

I went to her home. "Shalom eliechim."

"Eliechim shalom," she responded.

"I am Malchus, the servant of Caiaphas the High Priest."

"Oh, please come in," she said. "It is an honor to have the servant of the High Priest visit me. My husband and Caiaphas had some associations, but I have never met him."

Hoping to make this as easy as possible, I said, "He is the representative of God to us." I really believed Caiaphas was God's representative, but I was saying this to make my assignment easier. She seemed very nice, and I was a little hesitant about my task.

"May I get you some wine, a raisin cake perhaps?" she offered.

I wondered if she was being hospitable or was she genuinely pleased to have a visitor? I settled into a sturdy chair with a cushion. Some chairs are comfortable and you just accept the fact. This chair was so comfortable I was conscious of the comfort immediately. She stood by the chair's twin.

"No thank you," I responded. "I would like to get the business at hand completed."

"What is the 'business at hand?'" she queried.

I began, "It is about your husbands' declaration of this property as 'Corban' or dedicated to God." She was visibly shocked.

"Why, I knew nothing of this. Are you certain he did that? Did he not dedicate it to the Lord after I passed on, but not before? Surely he made some provision for me in this."

"No, I'm very sorry. He did not make any provisions about waiting. This property is 'Corban' now," I replied.

To my surprise and great relief, this woman, who had just received such shocking news, began to try to please me and Caiaphas as well as honor the memory of her husband. He had obviously taken good care of her, and she assumed that all people were honest and good like him.

"Must I move out?" she asked. "I had hoped to live out my days in this house. It is comfortable and well situated for me. I really prefer not to move."

"No, of course you may stay," I answered. "Caiaphas realized that you may wish to stay. He has instructed that if you like, you may purchase the house back at a price which is less than the market value since there would not be all the fees. Or, he suggested you could stay here as a renter for a suitable period of time."

"You are most kind," she said. I felt she really meant it. "How much would it cost to purchase the house again?"

"Twenty pieces of silver," I answered. She did not hesitate. "Please wait here. I will be right back."

She was gone for about half an hour. I don't know if she went out the back door to another location, or more likely dug up her savings from a place under the floor in her home. At last she returned with twenty pieces of silver. "Here you are, Malchus," she smiled. "Now I can finish my days here in peace. My husband left enough to make this possible. He was so good to me."

I was afraid she was going to go into a long discourse on her dead husband, and I wanted to leave as soon as possible. Cutting her short with some nice comments about both her and her husband, I left as quickly and as politely as I could.

When I was out of her sight, I began to run. I ran and jumped and whooped my way to Caiaphas. He was in his room at the Temple, alone. I rushed in and exclaimed, "Here. Here it is! The money, the money!"

With a surprised look, Caiaphas took the bag and without a word counted the twenty pieces of silver twice. He looked at me, looked at the silver and said, "Good job, Malchus. Good work. I'm impressed. I expected at least a couple days' delay.

Here. This is a bonus, a gift." He tossed three of the silver pieces to me. "Go spend it, and don't come back here for two or three days. No, don't come back until after Shabat."

When I told Bethany, she shrieked with delight, danced around the house clapping her hands over her head. We went to a favorite khan out in the wilderness near the Dead Sea. There were mineral baths, massage servants, and excellent food and accommodations for a price. We had a delicious time.

Many other assignments followed. Most all of them were more difficult to complete. I did a good job for Caiaphas, and advanced in responsibility and authority far beyond my years.

I enjoyed serving him. Caiaphas was within the law, or often his word was the law, so I served him well. Very seldom did I question my assignment, and when I did, Caiaphas usually took the time to explain why he was right. I never hesitated to do his work. If he was wrong, God would have to deal with him.

Caiaphas soon noticed and rewarded the intensity and zealousness with which I served him. At times he would encourage me to relax or take it easy, yet I knew he was pleased and liked my work.

My life was satisfying. I had a good wife and home. I had a job serving the representative of God. I was marked as the servant of the High Priest.

One day Caiaphas said, "Malchus, you are zealous for zealousness' sake."

"I am zealous for you great Caiaphas and your rightful place, for your divine assignment with the people of God," I responded.

"Maybe so, but I'm glad it's my ring in your ear. I wouldn't want you serving my enemies."

With a laugh I responded, "I will serve you well Caiaphas."

"You will serve me with zeal, Malchus," he corrected. "Sometimes it will be well, but sometimes your zealousness can be a real pain. However, I would rather have a couple of you wild stallions needing to be corralled now and then than a hundred mealy-mouthed opportunists. You're alright, Malchus."

"I will do anything for him," I vowed to myself that day.

* * *

I sat in on many meetings of the Sanhedrin, the ruling council of the elders of Israel. I couldn't sit in the circle of rulers, but just behind Caiaphas where he could summon me without interrupting the proceedings. It was exciting. My father sat just behind Annas, and many times we sat together.

The proceedings varied between laborious, terribly boring and technical, all the way to heated intensity, like a pot of food boiling over the fire. I loved the fiery sessions, and tolerated the others. The hottest issue for the Sanhedrin was the zealots.

Zealots are radicals who believe God ordained Israel for Jews, and Romans must be driven out no matter the cost. They inspired a patriotism in the Pharisees and a fear in the Sadducees. Every time a band of zealots stirred up the wrath of Rome, the Sanhedrin spent much time in emergency sessions.

A report had reached Caiaphas about a band of zealots in Joppa who were stirring up discontent and recruiting young men for their cause. He dispatched me to Joppa to investigate and bring a report. As was often the case, he wanted me to go undercover, this time posing as a buyer of property.

I decided to mix a holiday with business and take Bethany along. Our first born son, Jehoiada, was two years old by then, and my mother was elated at the chance to "spoil him." She sent us off with the admonition, "You two make some more babies for me."

Joppa is a beautiful town perched on rocky cliffs overlooking the Mediterranean Sea about a days' journey from Jerusalem. The harbor abounds with rocks, but is still used as the seaport for Jerusalem, just as it was when Hiram floated the timber there for the building of Solomon's Temple.

We fell in love with the people, the refreshing sea breezes and the beautiful rugged coast. We found housing with a widow named Dorcas who treated us like family. She and Bethany quickly became friends, and it seemed as if they had known each other for years. Whenever I returned from investigating properties or just poking around, they would be chattering like magpies. We attended the local synagogue with her and Bethany helped her with her sewing and visiting the poor.

Although buying property was only a pretense, we actually purchased a parcel of land about a ten minute walk south of town. It was perched on a finger of land with the ocean on three sides. We planned to build a vacation home there in spite of its impracticality for children. We were captured by the beauty and the dream of getting away like this. Besides, the price was only two pieces of silver.

My investigation confirmed to Caiaphas the reports about the zealots. Historically Joppa had been a place of turmoil and intrigue and it still festered. A large number of people hated the Romans with an intensity beyond that in Jerusalem. Fanaticism was easily stirred up, and a young man named Barabbas was a special trouble maker. At a share-your-meal dinner after the synagogue service, he even tried to recruit me. I feigned enough interest to keep him going and he pushed and manipulated with every zealot argument and condemnation of spineless Jews who made peace with the anti-God system. He appeared hard and mean and was looking for trouble with or without a cause. I was certain he wouldn't hesitate to kill anyone who opposed him. I identified him to Caiaphas as a troublemaker who needed to be watched.

* * *

Although Bethany and I promised each other to get away like this at least once a year, even twice we hoped, I was busy and she was pregnant, and the children kept us at home. It was almost two years before we made another trip, this time to the wilderness of Judea where a strange character claiming to be a prophet was drawing huge crowds. It was also to be business and pleasure, but the business took priority and a wedge was driven between Bethany and me that grew bigger and more ominous over the next three years.

CHAPTER FIVE

ROME

Cleomus barges into my cell, shocking me back to the present with his harshness. "Malchus, you said you were a cobbler so you can fix my sandals. The strap broke—here, fix it."

"Sure Cleomus," I respond, "but I need the small tool bag that's with my property. They took it from me when I arrived here."

"Just a minute," Cleomus grunts, and goes off to fetch my tools.

While he is gone, I pray about the situation and what I should do. Like Jesus did, I pray along the lines of a favorite Psalm: "My ear you have pierced. I am yours. Here I am O my God. I have come to do your will. What would you have me do in this?"

I hear a quiet response deep inside, "Give him your sandals."

The immediate internal responses are, "No way." "He wouldn't accept them." "That's stupid." "He'll think you're trying to buy him." I am learning to ignore these alien intrusions into my being. Prison was helping me sort out who was planting thoughts in my mind.

I smile and say, "Thank you Lord."

Cleomus is a long time in returning and I begin to torment myself with the cruel whip of "if only I had known." If only I had known when we went out to the wilderness to see John the Baptist. "If only I had known," is a destructive habit. The way it happened then, and the way it happens now, is the way it is.

it is. Self condemnation from, "if only I had known," has often troubled me.

JERUSALEM

I was excited with the prospects of taking Bethany on another trip. Caiaphas wanted a first hand account of the happenings at the Jordan river, and I was to be his eyes and ears. All of Judea was buzzing about this so called prophet, John the baptizer. He was the main topic of conversation wherever people gathered. At the wells, when the women drew water, at the marketplace, at the shops and industries, and of course at the meetings of the Sanhedrin, this John was discussed.

This time Bethany and I took the children. Huge crowds were making the day long trip to the Jordan and there was a carnival like atmosphere all along the way. There were vendors along the roadside selling raisin cakes, and figs, and various fruits and breads. My son, Jehoiada, and I spent some great times together. I carried him on my shoulders some of the time and we would wander slightly off the paths to explore. At his age everything fascinated him.

He saw a leaf that had changed color and shrieked for joy. "Oh Abba, Abba look." He clutched the leaf in his tiny hand as if he had discovered a great treasure. Next it was a stick and then a stone with unusual markings. Soon I would have to carry these things spilling from his tiny hands, and add it to the growing bag of "treasure."

"Jehoiada, let's leave some of these beautiful things for others to discover too," I suggested.

"No! This is mine. I want to keep it," he defiantly answered.

How much this little boy was like me shocked me, and so did how much I was like him, in hoarding my treasure stash. Oh well, such is the way of all men, and I liked my growing stash of treasure. I had a good time with my son, and promised myself to spend more time with Jehoiada. Like the well meaning promise to get away with Bethany, this too was subordinated to the will of Caiaphas and my growing responsibilities.

Because of the children, we didn't push ourselves to get to the Jordan in one day. We also wanted to enjoy our little holiday. About midafternoon, we saw a large cluster of booths and cooking stations where you could rent a shelter for the night and buy a nice meal. Our people are known to be enterprising. Whenever an opportunity to help each other, and make some money in the process arises, this characteristic is evident.

We stopped and picked a nice shelter at the back, nearest the wilderness. The cluster of booths was near the descent into the Jordan Valley, but because of the oppressive heat in the valley, even at night, and the abundance of wild animals there, the preferred resting place was right here. There were several hundred booths, plus space for those who slept in the open, or carried their own coverings.

We paid for water and the use of the bathing booths, and I had the experience of taking Jehoiada with me into the men's area and giving him his cleansing. Other people were there, pouring water over each other's heads. This frightened Jehoiada. He did not want that water poured over him and began to fuss. I started to get angry, and then thought better of it. He was only a small boy on the biggest adventure of his young life. So after soaping him up I started a water fight.

I put my hand in the water and flecked a few drops at him. He looked amazed as if to say, "What's happening?" I smiled mischievously and did it again. I grinned and did it once more. He wasn't sure whether to scream and cry, or get his hands in the water and get me. He made a little movement and I flinched as if I were afraid of him flicking water at me. That was the cue he needed, and his little hands scooped up as much water as they could hold and he threw it at me. I yowled and moaned and threw more on him, being careful not to get it in his eyes.

Soon water erupted all around us as we frantically splashed and threw it on one another. When our water supply was gone, we were laughing and enjoying ourselves and were also squeaky clean. Jehoiada was now a seasoned bather, and I had had a great time. Some of our bath neighbors enjoyed our fun, but others were upset with us. I didn't care what they thought.

At supper, Jehoiada didn't eat much. "I told you not to buy him all those honey cakes and then those raisin cakes," Bethany scolded. "His stomach can't handle that many sweets, and now he won't get his nourishment." I smiled and winked at Jehoiada, just ignoring Bethany's remarks.

The children were fast asleep soon after dusk. Groups of travellers were talking, but Bethany and I didn't want to wander off to visit with others lest the children wake up alone and be afraid. It had not yet cooled down so we lay half in and half out of the booth, with our upper bodies out in the night air. We lay close together on our backs looking up into the incredible display of stars.

"It's majestic, isn't it?" I was not asking as much as just commenting.

"What?" Bethany asked.

"The stars, the beauty and the grandeur of it. It makes me feel small and insignificant."

"It makes me feel good and cozy," Bethany responded, "to think that the God who made all of this has chosen us to be his own special possession." Bethany moved her head to rest on my arm and went on. "I wonder why he chose us over others?"

I responded quickly, "You can go crazy trying to answer that question. God just chose us. He has his own reasons, but we are most fortunate. We have the Temple, the High Priest, the law of Moses and the tradition of the elders."

"What's it like, Malchus, being so close to the High Priest? Is he different in a way you can see, or is he just like others," Bethany asked?

I laughed, feeling warm and good about my high position with Caiaphas, and said, "He is just a man like any of us, but his office gives him a power and mystique that makes him different. When he speaks, to me it's almost the same as if God speaks. I know he is not God, but he is the closest to God. He is the chief representative of God on earth."

Bethany made a "mmmhmmm" sound and put her head on my arm.

We went on talking for hours. Sometimes we discussed big important things, and some of the time we just chatted. We had not talked like this for a long time, and we promised each other we would do it more often. I had no idea it would be more than three years before we would feel this close again.

* * *

Awaking to the smells of baking bread and the sound of hungry children, we dressed quickly. While Bethany nursed Sarah, Jehoiada and I went to buy some of that great smelling bread. We bought enough for the journey and the time at the Jordan. We ate several pieces by the time we got back to the booth. Bread is never better than when it is still warm.

Back on the road I began to slip away from my role as husband and father, and became more the servant of the High Priest. I was here to investigate John the baptizer and his effect on the people. The focus of my thinking centered more and more on the people, and I tried to sense what they were feeling. I noticed that the travellers going to the Jordan were happy and expectant, while the ones returning were somber and serious. The heat was stifling, but more than that, a heaviness and sense of foreboding began to settle on me, as we came to the place John was baptizing and preaching.

The reports that "everyone was going out there" were not exaggerated. Making our way through the milling crowds was difficult. Hundreds and hundreds sat on the sloping bank of the Jordan where they could see and hear. Others moved about like a sea of people. The river was narrow at this point, only twenty or thirty cubits wide. The opposite shore was a rocky cliff.

John, the one they called "the baptist," perched on a rock on the other side of the river, was eating. It looked to me like he was eating locusts. He had what appeared to be a pile of them and a container of honey. He would dip the insects in the honey and chew them up. I was disgusted watching him eat.

John, reminding me of a bear I had seen a few years before—big and hairy and loud—was wearing a garment of camel's hair and a leather sash around the middle. I had never seen anyone wear such an outfit. His hair and beard were uncut and blew in the breeze. He seemed oblivious to what he was eating, where he was and what he was doing.

I was anxious to investigate, and told Bethany to watch the children. She looked at me and scowled, but said she understood. She realized I was determined.

Wandering through the crowd, I mentally noted some of the people present. I identified dignitaries from all over Judea and Galilee from their visits to Caiaphas. I just moved casually about, pretending not to recognize anyone. Right at the water's edge was a group of scribes and pharisees that I knew too well to ignore. As I greeted them, the crowd's attention turned to John.

He shook himself as if waking from a nap, washed the honey and locust parts from his beard and hands in the river, and turned to face directly into our group. I'm certain he growled before he roared his message. "You bunch of snakes. Who warned you to flee from the wrath of God to come upon you? Repent because the Kingdom of heaven is near."

I was enraged. Who does he think he is? He is deluded. He acts as if he was Elijah, and not answerable to the God-given leaders. We have the Temple and the High Priest from the line of Aaron and Levi. He is the one who needs to repent—he is blaspheming the authority of God.

John continued talking about the one who was coming, who supposedly was here now, and who would touch us with the fire of God. People from the crowd called out questions to him. His answers were the same as his message. Change! Turn away from sin! Repent! Then he ordered the people to be baptized by him, to wash away their sins he said, and to prepare for the coming kingdom.

Who does he think he is, telling us such things? But even more incredible was the fact that hundreds of people responded to him and began wading into the river. I noticed in the crowd old Nicodemus, one of the Sanhedrin. Another, Joseph of Arimathea, even went into the water for baptism. I felt these men were traitors to our religious system, and I decided to go and tell Caiaphas at once.

I found Bethany and the children where I had left them. They had been joined by another family who were neighbors back home. I didn't know them well, but Bethany and the wife were close. I almost ignored our neighbors and said, "Bethany, we must return immediately, and we must hurry."

Bethany protested that the children couldn't make it in a rushed trip. Our neighbor suggested that Bethany and the children stay with them another day and he would watch over both families. I quickly agreed. Giving Bethany some money, and saying a quick good-bye, I was back on the road in only a few minutes.

Caiaphas was as upset as I had been when he heard my report. "Malchus," he said, "I want you to follow very carefully what's happening with this man John. He is dangerous and we are at a distinct disadvantage in dealing with him, because of the fickle crowds. God willing, this will all come to nothing, but I want to know everything!"

I accepted Caiaphas' charge with determination and pride. It was a sacred trust to defend and preserve the tradition of the elders. I looked forward to the assignment and began plotting immediately how I might get rid of this John. The way he flies off and condemns people should make it easy. Surely he'll go too far and I'll trap him like a bird in a net, as I thought, I smashed my fist into my palm.

When Bethany and the children returned, they were tired from the journey and the children were cranky. I was glad to see them and my joy spilled over in thanks to God. Soon after the evening meal, the children were bedded down, the lamps were lit, and we had our chance to talk. My peace was shattered quickly.

"Oh Malchus," she began, "if only you could have stayed another day. It was awesome. I can hardly describe it. John's words were like a hammer breaking the hardness in my heart."

"Come on, Bethany, you have one of the most tender hearts I've ever seen. He didn't break any hardness, he just trapped you with his words."

"No, Malchus!" she insisted. "He helped me turn to the Messiah." My mouth fell open. She continued, "The very next day, Jesus of Nazareth came back from the wilderness. John had baptized him six weeks ago. When he came to the place John was baptizing, John stopped speaking and pointed at him. 'Look! The lamb of God that takes away the sin of the world.'"

"What!" I exclaimed.

"Yes," she continued. "John said God had told him that the one he saw the Spirit descend upon is the Messiah. After he baptized Jesus, John saw the Spirit descend and remain on him, and he even heard the voice of God say, 'This is my beloved Son.' Some of John's followers went to talk to Jesus, but we had to leave. Oh, Malchus, it's so exciting. God is setting up his kingdom now."

Angry at myself for taking her to the Jordan, and angry at her for letting John dupe her, I responded slowly and forcefully, "Bethany, you're acting like a fool. You had a nice experience and a pleasant trip. The hope and future of Israel is in the institutions God has established and favored. The High Priest, The Sanhedrin, The Temple. If this is the Messiah, these God-ordained leaders will tell us about it. If they don't, I don't want you preaching at me about some Nazarene. Do you understand?"

There was silence. Bethany stared at the floor.

"Bethany," I demanded, "do you understand?"

She looked at me with tears streaming down her face and nodded her head.

CHAPTER SIX

JERUSALEM

I took two scribes, experts in the law, and went back to the Jordan to deal with this baptizer. I left quickly because the issue had to be dealt with immediately. Actually, I also wanted some space between Bethany and me.

I no longer knew how to talk to her or relate to her. In our few exchanges she was submissive to me in every way, but it was dutiful and cold. This one who used to look at me with respect and admiration, now looked at me with a distance. It was as if I was looking through a window, while remaining outside.

Being around her was too uncomfortable. I felt like I was not a man anymore, not respected or admired. It was a relief to be back on the road, and to have these scribes do my bidding. It made me feel important and powerful. I felt otherwise at home—tolerated and powerless. We went straight to the Jordan without stopping.

I arranged a small table for the scribes, away from the crowd, but where they could still see and hear clearly. I instructed these lawyers to get down anything John said that was controversial or dangerous. I said, "Make sure you get it written the way he said it so we can get witnesses. I don't want any loose ends in dealing with this man. Do you understand?" They assured me they did. I kept a close check over their work. I wanted to make sure they did exactly as I commanded.

While they transcribed the messages, I listened to John preach. I held an ongoing argument with him in my mind. I either refuted each point or dismissed it as ridiculous. The more our debate went on, the more hardened and closed I became.

We stayed at the Jordan for three days. When I saw various acquaintances there, I smiled and politely conversed without saying anything. In the service of Caiaphas, I had become an expert at masking my sentiments. But in the evening, after John had finished his "show," I would carefully go over the content of his preaching with the scribes. There were many innuendos and outright judgments against all manner of people, including Annas and Caiaphas. Although we could make a lot of trouble for him from this alone, it wouldn't accomplish as much as what I had in mind.

My issue surfaced the third day. John said, "It is wrong, it is illegal, for that fox, Herod, to have his brother's wife. Just because Caesar appointed this half Jew to rule, he is not exempt from the law of Moses. Herodias is Philip's wife, and Herod may not take her as his wife." This was it! No one could deny he said it. No matter if he was right or wrong, now I had him in a trap that was also useful in putting pressure on Herod. Any weakening of Herod or the Roman Governor in Judea, would strengthen the position of Caiaphas, and thereby the rule of God.

Upon returning, I reported to Caiaphas before going home. He listened carefully, then said, "Malchus, there's an official delegation from the Sanhedrin going out to question John. Their questions and endless debates will take an intolerable amount of time to resolve. But, if you can cause Herod to take action against John, we will be relieved of a very difficult and unpopular problem. John must be silenced, and it's better that Herod do it rather than the Sanhedrin. Take one of the scribes with you and go see Herod at once."

I felt smug when I finally saw Bethany. Hurrying about the house, my thoughts were on the removal of John, the discrediting of his country Messiah and the return of my wife to the tradition of the elders. Wanting to leave as quickly as possible, I mumbled a good-bye, but Bethany said, "God go with you, my husband."

Herod had been spending a great deal of time in Perea at his palace in Machaerus, but our intelligence told me he was presently at Tiberius in Galilee. For a fleeting moment I considered visiting white-haired Asaph, but I didn't want to tell him about Bethany, and I fretted he would guess the cause of my tension.

The scribe and I rode donkeys and made good time. Rather than go through Samaria and risk trouble with the riff-raff who lived there, we veered to the east and crossed the Jordan twice. I didn't like lawyers, and avoided conversation with this one.

When he asked me a question about Herod and Philip, I gave a brief overview in as curt a manner as possible. Herod Antipas ruled Galilee in the north, and Perea east of the Dead Sea. Like his father, Herod the Great, he was a builder and had constructed several palaces and forts throughout his regions. When Herod the Great died, Antipas was one of only three sons who survived his father's insane rage and jealousy. His brother Archelaus received Judea, Idumea and Samaria. He was supposed to get the crown, but Caesar never conferred it on him. His brother Philip was named tetrarch of the areas east of the Jordan.

Herod the Great carved out for himself the number two position of power in the Roman Empire. Our fathers hated him even though he rebuilt the Temple to an incredible splendor. He was only a half Jew, yet clung to the title, "King of the Jews" with messianic fervor. He killed everyone who challenged his rule, whether nobles, priests, wives, sons or even innocent children at Bethlehem. Everyone who was a threat to his throne went to the grave by the hand of this murderous monarch.

When he died, and Antipas, Philip and Archelaus started their reigns, we sent a delegation to Caesar to request that Judea not have a king but be added to Rome's province of Syria. Caesar went ahead and appointed Archelaus ethnarc of half the country in spite of our request, and even promised to give him the title if he deserved it.

Nine years later, my father went to Rome with another delegation and this time they succeeded in having Archelaus removed. They got the support of Quirinius in Syria and so, for the last twenty years, the power of life and death in Judea rested with the Roman procurator. Since the procurator stays in Caesarea most of the time, the real power to rule rests with

Annas, Caiaphas and the Sanhedrin, unless things get out of hand. We haven't tested this newcomer procurator, Pontius Pilate, at least not yet.

Herod Antipas and Philip had been crafty enough to keep their rule, and continue their decadent lifestyles. I was trying to chip away some of their power base, and give it to Caiaphas.

The scribe was livid from my demeaning treatment, and we rode for hours in silence. From the mouth of the Jordan we followed the western shore of the Sea of Galilee up to Tiberius. The Sea of Galilee displayed a refreshing panorama of all the shades of blue and green. It is magnificent, I thought, but not as beautiful and rugged as my beloved Joppa.

Riding past the fertile fields, fruit orchards and lush grazing land, it was easy to see why these Galileans were more settled and peaceful than we were in Judea. The road to Tiberius was pleasant and the view of the city, spectacular. The fading sun colored the sky a hazy yellow as we rode past the mineral baths at the south end of the city. A three mile wall surrounds this creation of Herod with its huge imposing palace. Although the city itself is small, there are enough residents to serve Herod's high living style while he is in residence.

Between the gate and the entrance to the palace we met every sort of low life. Propositioned by prostitutes, offered merchandise at prices below market value, and approached to buy protection for our mules while in Tiberius, my scribe was shocked. He asked, "What's with these people, Malchus? I've never seen such a disgrace."

I reminded him, "Herod built this city on a graveyard. It is unclean, and proper Jews won't live here. These people patronize Herod and his guests only because Herod's justice is swift and cruel. Any of our own countrymen who happen to come here better not come alone, and keep a hand on their purse."

"I don't like this place," he continued. "Let's get out of here as soon as we can."

"Don't worry," I told him. "We are on a mission for Caiaphas, and any evil here is covered by the godliness of our task." I wanted to have a mineral bath, a rub down and a few days' rest. I hoped this religious freak wouldn't spoil my plans. I was changing.

Any onlookers could tell my companion was a scribe, and with the ring in my ear we were not treated with the respect our mission deserved. I rarely corrected my servant image, since the acceptance of average people allowed me to gain helpful insights. The attendant at the entrance to the palace obviously thought we should be coming to the servants' door in the back.

"What do you want," he gruffly asked?

"Take our donkeys to the barn and see that they are cared for," I ordered.

He was taken aback, but we immediately went up the stairs and ignored his protests. Fifteen stairs ran the entire length of the palace. At the top were six massive columns and a portico also the width of the entire building. Several doors opened onto the portico, and the main entrance doors in the center were open. The scribe seemed hesitant and fearful, but I walked right through the open doors into a magnificent reception area. Polished marble was everywhere and statues of various emperors and Roman deities lined the walls. I had been exposed to such paganism before, but the scribe was shocked.

Another attendant rushed to stop us, but before he could say a word, I said, "We are here from the High Priest to meet with Herod. Give him this." I handed him the letter from Caiaphas.

With some uncertainty and obvious confusion he said, "Wait right here." We took a seat on one of the benches along the side of the hall.

After a few minutes he returned with two other attendants. "Herod is entertaining this evening and cannot see you until morning. You are most welcome here, Malchus," he said. "These men will show you to your rooms." Jews who served Romans were uncomfortable around scribes, and this servant was obviously distraught at the presence of this expert in the law of Moses. Although I had learned to cope with this scribe, I was grateful we were being separated.

My room was on the third floor with a balcony overlooking the Sea of Galilee, although while here I should call it Lake Tiberius. There was a beautiful silver bowl filled with grapes, figs, dates and apples, matching platters of meats and also breads and pastries. A pitcher of excellent wine completed the spread. A sunken tub was being filled with hot water by an entourage of servants. I ate some of the dainties on the balcony, and then soaked my tired body in the luxurious tub. A servant entered and provided towels, a vigorous rub down, and then an oil rub. I heard female voices drift through the open balcony. There was giggling and the sounds of revelry and teasing. I tried to hear more, but the good wine, the long trip, the hot bath and the servant's soothing rubbing sent me into a deep sleep that lasted till the fourth watch of the night.

I awoke with my recurring childhood nightmare. The curtains were flapping straight towards me and even on my bed I could feel the wind whipped rain. Struggling to close the balcony doors I was frightened by the turbulence of the Sea. It's hard to believe that an inland body of water could become so furious. "Even the Sea is angry at me," I muttered.

I tried to sleep, but it was no use. Thoughts of Bethany and Jehoiada, of Caiaphas and John the baptizer, and the meeting with Herod harassed my mind. It was all so confusing. At times like this, it seems so hopeless. How will I ever get back with Bethany? How will we ever get through this terrible impasse now that she is rejecting the tradition of the elders?

I finally got out of the bed and sat by the balcony doors staring into the darkness. The unrest of wind and water seemed to draw my own anxiety into itself and calm me, but as I was watching, the storm suddenly stopped. It was as though a farmer had turned a watercourse from one channel to another. One minute the channel of turbulence and rage was boiling, and in the next few moments the scene was calm and peaceful.

When Herod sent for us it was midmorning. I met the scribe in the hall near Herod's reception room. He was trembling and perspiring and said, "Well, here we go."

I assured him that it would be fine and to let me do the talking unless he was addressed specifically. He was relieved.

The attendant opened the doors and accompanied us into a luxurious room. Everyone referred to Herod as king. He even spoke of his tetrarchy as a kingdom. He was seated on a regal chair on a raised platform. Courtesy suggested that those appearing before him make some sign of respect or obeisance. I nodded in a proper show of respect while the scribe stood stiff necked and unyielding.

"Welcome, Malchus. What brings you to Tiberius?" Herod asked.

I responded, "Your Highness, it's good to see you again looking so well. Caiaphas sends you his greetings and dispatched us here on a most troubling matter. Caiaphas is concerned for your welfare and reputation, King Herod. When a certain self-appointed prophet began defaming you, he sent us here with a report."

Herod leaned forward in his chair and asked, "Well, what is it? Who is this person and what is he saying?"

I replied, "He is called John the baptizer, and is drawing huge crowds out to the Jordan where he viciously attacks the tradition of the elders. He has also condemned you, King Herod."

"What? What is he saying?" demanded Herod.

"Perhaps you would like to hear exactly what he said?" I asked. "The scribe here has an official transcript of his tirades against you."

"Yes, yes. Read it scribe," Herod said.

The scribe read the report, and Herod responded, "Is this true Malchus?"

"Yes, your highness," I responded. "I went to investigate and heard him myself."

Herod was livid. He reached for the report, and the scribe immediately handed it over. Herod dismissed the scribe, "That will be all. Return to Jerusalem." Then the tetrarch turned to me and said, "Malchus, I would like to talk with you some more." Dismissing his own attendants, he led me to a large conference-type table at the side of the room where we could speak.

"The fool," he snapped. "The God damned fool. He's putting a twig to his nose, and I'm liable to drive it into his twisted brain." Then Herod was quiet for a moment while the red color that consumed his entire head was isolated to the sides of his neck. "What do you think about this Malchus? I'm sure you've thought about it and have some recommendations."

"Well sir," I said, "I think it would be unwise to just go and arrest him, because of the people. He is tremendously popular with the crowds. So, unless there were good cause at the very moment, arresting him or killing him could spark rebellion."

Herod nodded to himself and I continued, "The crowds are a real cross section of the populace. There were even Roman soldiers there asking him questions. Some of them were baptized."

"Incredible," Herod remarked.

"Under these circumstances, you could send a delegation of your own. If a spokesman asked the right questions, I am certain this John would incriminate himself with these same lies. At that point he could be arrested, and the crowds would have no recourse because of the offense."

Herod seemed pleased with my counsel and said, "If I follow this plan, could you stay on a few days and give some coaching to my men? Tell them what to expect and how to trap him?"

I was delighted. "I would be happy to serve you in any way I can, sir," I lied.

Herod sent for some food and we ate together at that same table. During the conversation he asked about the affairs in Jerusalem, and what this Pontius Pilate was really like. They had not yet met, and Herod knew very little about him. In an effort to paint a picture of a man who thought Rome should rule the world with its own commanders, I gave Herod selective, biased information. I implied that Pilate believed regional tetrarchies like Herod's were not in the best interest of Caesar. I was careful to stay within the boundaries of known facts and of my own personal opinions. That way, Caiaphas would not be implicated should Pilate and Herod ever compare notes. I was confident that the seeds of distrust had been firmly planted. I hated Herod and everything he stood for.

For two days I enjoyed the baths and excessive provisions of Herod's hospitality. I ached for Bethany, and yet grew angrier because of our division and her foolish enchantment with this soon-to-be-removed prophet, and his so-called messiah.

When I returned, I was smug about what would happen to this baptizer, but was wise enough not to tell Bethany. The tension with Bethany continued to grow. I would hear her laugh with others, but found myself on the outside of any meaningful conversation. Once, when I returned home unexpectedly, she was on her knees praying with the neighbor. They seemed nervous and embarrassed to see me. Somehow, I felt attacked by their actions.

Bethany submitted to all of my sexual advances, but no longer was it two people becoming one flesh, it was now a man satisfying himself with the body of this woman. My resentment mounted every time I lowered myself to use her in that way. I felt like less of a man. The wedge between us drove us further apart.

At times our relationship seemed hopeless. How could this fanatical messiah business ever be reconciled to our religion and traditions? I probably would have given up hope, but service to Caiaphas was centered in getting rid of Jesus. Once I had done a good job for Caiaphas and this Jesus of Nazareth was removed, my wife would be restored. Or so I thought.

CHAPTER SEVEN

ROME

Cleomus finally returns with my bag of tools and some scrap pieces of leather. He mutters about being busy and demands, "How long will this take? I don't have all night."

"Cleomus," I respond, "I'd like to give you my sandals, and fix yours for me. If God should intervene and get me out of here, I can make some more later. In the meantime, I can use these."

Cleomus is stunned. My sandals are probably the finest he has ever seen. He slowly takes them, with a strange tenderness. As he puts them on, he says, "No one has ever given me anything." He stands up and tests them, and his expression clearly indicates they feel good on his feet.

He stands for a moment looking at me. I am certain he wants to thank me, but receiving gifts and saying thanks is unfamiliar ground for Cleomus. It seems like a dark cloud comes over his face and he says, "Hey prisoner, you're a slaughtered swine in two days anyway. If not, you can wear my old ones that you fix."

As he walks off I pray, "Thank you Lord. You do everything just right. Let your love for Cleomus come through me, and through those sandals on his feet. May they constantly remind him that he is loved." I laugh out loud at the mental picture I have of the warmth of the love of God radiating up from his feet and going through Cleomus' entire being.

I remember how I had resisted the love of God and his gift of Jesus. It's hard, at least it was hard for me, to receive a genuine gift. I always wanted to be the giver, the hero, the person in charge. Even when Bethany opened the door of her soul to me during those difficult years, I resisted any overture I thought might cost me my position of being right.

JERUSALEM

Caiaphas was pleased with what happened in our covert operation to get rid of John the baptizer. Herod's soldiers arrested John and there was no trouble from the crowd. Even John's own disciples accepted the situation since John was so adamant about Herod's sin. My plan had been perfectly executed. The pressure was off the Sanhedrin and we could now concentrate on Jesus. The distrust I had managed to plant between Herod and Pilate proved to be an extra bonus, and a rift was growing between them. My position with Caiaphas grew stronger; I was his trusted right hand, and was received as such by most.

The problems with Jesus, however, grew daily. He itinerated throughout Judea and Galilee, and even into Samaria. Huge crowds were attracted to him, just like they were to John. We wondered why such strange characters drew large crowds. Many claimed they were healed of sickness and disease by Jesus. We attributed this to the phenomenon that weak, senseless people wanted to think they were healed. Daily we received reports that Jesus was the Messiah, or claimed to be the Messiah; some even asked us if he was the Messiah. It was a busy time, but I was a respected leader. At home, however, it was another story.

Since the arrest of John, my relationship with Bethany continued to spiral downwards. I found it easier to stay away from home. When we did talk, it was painfully obvious that she was a devoted follower of Jesus. With a vengeance, I buried myself in service to Caiaphas. When I was angry at Bethany, I struck out at her by doing everything possible to get rid of Jesus. This unbearable situation continued on for two more years.

By the Feast of Tabernacles of the third year of Jesus' public exposure, we, Jewish leaders, were determined to kill him. The common people grew more and more excited about his teaching and legendary miracles. At first Jesus didn't come to Jerusalem for the festival, but silver-haired Asaph did. Since I did not have to coordinate the efforts to trap Jesus, I was forced to spend time with the family.

My family joined with relatives from all over Israel and built booths at my father's house. I was nervous and irritable. The meeting was inevitable, and soon Asaph took me aside and asked what was wrong. I excused my behavior with some comments about the pressures on Caiaphas and me because of Jesus, and the tensions mounting throughout all Israel. I mentioned that I could not have been here with the family if Jesus had come to the festival.

I respected Asaph as much as I did anyone, except of course Caiaphas, so it really shocked me when he said, "What if this Jesus is the Messiah?"

I threw back my standard answer, "If he is, the High Priest and the other God-ordained leaders will tell us."

Very gently Asaph said, "Malchus, I am a God-ordained priest of the line of Aaron, and I tell you, 'I don't know as yet who this Nazarene really is.' You would do well not to get locked into a premature position."

As Asaph and I were talking, and some of the families were beginning to prepare the evening meal, a messenger came from Caiaphas. "I'm sorry to interrupt your time with your family Malchus, but Caiaphas needs you right away," he said. I welcomed the excuse to leave, made some quick apologies, and left immediately.

It seems Jesus had come after all, and suddenly appeared in the Temple that afternoon. He was teaching that none of us keep the law of Moses, but if anyone chose to do the will of God, that person would know that the teaching Jesus was bringing was from God. I thought, "What arrogance!"

The Sanhedrin met a long time that evening trying to come to a resolution about Jesus and to set a definite course of action. After the meeting was dismissed, I sat in on a strategy session with Annas, Caiaphas and some leading Pharisees. My assignment was to oversee the Temple guards and station them where they could quickly arrest Jesus if he created a problem.

Each morning, during the Feast of Tabernacles, an honored priest filled a golden pitcher with water from the fountain of Siloah. In a solemn procession, he then brought it to the Altar of Burnt Sacrifice. There, together with a pitcher of wine from the drink offering, he poured out the water into two perforated flat bowls. The trumpets sounded, and all the people sang, "With joy you will draw water from the wells of salvation."

The next day, the last and greatest day of the feast, the High Priest himself led the procession and poured out the golden pitchers symbolizing the water our fathers drank from the rock at Meribah. I was inspired by the beauty and holiness of the action. Caiaphas led the procession with solemnity and dignity. This was the high point of the feast. The trumpets sounded, the people sang, when suddenly our ceremony was shattered by the loud voice of the rabbi from Nazareth.

Jesus was standing on something so he could be seen and heard above the huge crowd. Those of us who hated him, and those who followed him, both heard him say, "If anyone is thirsty, let him come to me and drink. Whoever believes in me, as the scripture has said, 'streams of living water will flow from within him.'"

A tremendous uproar followed. Some were shouting, "Jesus! Jesus!" and others of us, "Heresy! Arrest him. Arrest him!" The uproar continued, but no arrests were made. I summoned the guards to the official quarters of the High Priest.

Caiaphas and Annas were already there. I approached them with the commander of the guard and his men following right behind me. When we came together, I deliberately turned and struck the commander full in the face with the back of my hand. "How dare you allow this false prophet to disrupt the festival and interrupt the sacred pouring of water by the High Priest," I demanded.

Caiaphas was livid with rage. He asked the commander, "Why didn't you arrest him?"

The commander was wise enough to keep silent, but some of the men began saying, "No one ever spoke the way this man does."

At that point, anything could have happened. The meeting had to be stopped. Our common enemy was out in the Temple, not here in the chambers. I took hold of the commander's tunic and spoke into his face, "Take your men back out there and position yourselves where you can see me. When I raise a fist, arrest him." Then I continued loud enough for all the soldiers to hear, "If you do not obey me, I will have you beaten and removed from command. Do you understand?"

"Yes sir," he responded.

"And the same goes for each of you men," I added.

I watched the guards disperse throughout the crowd, and positioned myself at the outside wall of the Court of the Gentiles, where Jesus was teaching. The crowd circled him, and came between us, so that he did not see me. Yet as he talked, I felt he was talking to me. I was terribly uncomfortable, but attributed it to his power over the crowds. I was firmly resolved to stop him.

I knew well this man was dangerous. The Pharisees had already set two traps for him that day but he completely turned the traps against them. This was no village carpenter, but a brilliant rabbi. He was a formidable foe.

Jesus was still there in the Court of the Gentiles. He was teaching his followers, and also answering and arguing with his opponents at the same time. The argument came to the place where Jesus actually spoke the words that those contending with him were children of the devil. I heard him say, "I tell you the truth, before Abraham was born, I myself, 'I AM!'"

There it was. That was certainly enough. Jesus actually claimed to be the I AM who spoke to Moses at the burning bush. Some of the people took up stones to kill him, and I signaled the guards with a nod of the head and a throwing motion with my arm to let the crowd stone him.

I quickly realized that stoning was impossible because of the huge crowd pressing on every side. I frantically began to signal the guards to arrest Jesus, but it was too late. He slipped away. Somehow he managed to elude us all.

For the next six months I had no personal contact with Jesus or his followers, but my life seemed to revolve around him. Caiaphas wanted access to everything about Jesus, and he relied on me to have all the information. I sent out spies and informants and ordered reports from a variety of sources. At times I thought I would drown in a sea of reports. I wearied of reading about Jesus, about his followers, about his family, about his disciples, about his trip to Bethany and the supposed raising of Lazarus, about his supporters, about where he was, about who in the Sanhedrin was sympathetic to him, and about anything else that some hired scribe thought was worthy of note.

I vowed that I would be ready for him at Passover, and that he would not get away again.

He did not get away, and neither did I.

CHAPTER EIGHT

ROME

As Caesar's birthday draws closer, the pressure here in the prison increases tremendously. I am jolted back to this present reality by the screams of a fellow captive. He shrieks and cries out, "No! No! Caesar is Lord! Caesar is Lord! Caesar is Lord! Caesar is Lord! Caesar is Lord!"

It is devastating. We all say, "No brother. Jesus is Lord! It's all right. Don't give up! You can make it!" But it is too late. He has cracked and he seems to hear nothing. Then we chant, "Jesus is Lord! "Jesus Is Lord!" At first only a few of us, but soon twenty or thirty prisoners joined the refrain. It is strong and powerful, but the defector keeps up his demented screaming and crying.

Several guards rush to his cell. Cleomus, arriving last, barks, "Get him out of here. And the rest of you shut-up." Two of the guards take his upper arms and drag off the still screaming, broken shell of a man. Another guard begins striking every prisoner he can reach with the butt end of a spear he is carrying. The sudden violent attack stops the chanting.

Soon, however, a soft refrain begins to permeate the prison as we sing one of our favorite songs, "Jesus reigns! Jesus reigns! He has broken death's strong grip and Jesus reigns!" We have learned that if we sing very softly, the guards do not disturb us. The softness and the hushed voices add to the power and blessing of this affirmation in song. I feel the vibrant presence of the Holy Spirit, and am deeply comforted.

My conviction to remain true and faithful to Jesus is strengthened. I vow never again to be among those who oppose

Jesus. "Oh Father," I pray, "give me grace to be faithful to You and Your Kingdom."

JERUSALEM

As that fateful Passover approached, we Jewish leaders slept less and ate many meals while we plotted and planned to stop Jesus. The stormy sessions constantly erupted in angry shouts. Things of no consequence at other times now evoked arguments, and on several occasions we had to protect individuals from physical blows. Two of our senior members tried to hit each other with their staffs. We planned many ingenious traps to catch Jesus, and I was certain he would not escape us. We set up the situations to discredit Jesus and give us justifiable reasons to get rid of him.

Finally, there was unity among the differing factions of the Sanhedrin in the common effort of ridding Israel of Jesus. Even the Pharisees had plotted a trap with the Herodians to catch him on the tax issue. What an alliance, they hate each other!

We thought we were ready. We thought we could trap him and arrest him quickly and quietly. We were wrong.

Jesus came into Jerusalem like a king who had conquered the nation. Looking back, it was more like a king who had set the nation free. He rode a donkey, a plain ordinary donkey, and yet everything about him was kingly: he held his head like a monarch; he sat on the donkey like an emperor; and he received the accolades of the people like a benevolent ruler. The whole procession was regal. Caesar in Rome would have been pleased with such a parade and such expressions from the people. At the time I perceived him as proud, arrogant, usurping priestly authority, and dangerous.

The people here in the city and those along the route cheered and waved branches. Some placed their cloaks on the road so that Jesus rode on a carpet of clothing into the city. The huge crowd followed him and shouted things that should be said only to the Messiah. The people were like a frenzied army with the taste of victory. Our task was going to be harder than we had planned.

Then, to make matters worse for us, Jesus went into the Temple and stirred up the rabble. He turned over the tables of the money changers. We subsidized the operations of the Temple with a percentage of the profits. The law required the worshippers to pay the temple tax, but since they came from all over the world they did not have the suitable coins.

Jesus didn't spare the animal sellers either. Again, since it was difficult for these travelers to get the lamb for the Passover, we provided a tidy little operation that made them available here at the site, for a price, of course.

The crowds cheered while Jesus overturned tables and spilled coins everywhere. The people laughed as the animals bleated and scampered throughout the temple area. They were thrilled. They never liked what we were doing and the confusion pleased them. The money changers, vendors, suppliers of the animals, scribes, priests, Pharisees and Sadducees stood apart from the crowds, shaking their fists and shouting curses on Jesus. Jesus then said, "It is written, 'My house shall be called a house of prayer, but you are making it a den of robbers.'"

Children were shouting, "Hosanna to the Son of David." This was so grievous that some of our leaders, without even taking counsel, challenged him right on the spot. That was a mistake. Jesus, to the delight of the crowd, said, "If the children don't praise me, the stones will." He then left the city for the night, clearly the victor in the day's battle.

We, leaders, immediately took counsel together. The issue of phenomenal public support for Jesus had to be considered. From all the possible courses of action, we decided to concentrate on two confrontations for the following day. First, we will confront him with the question of authority. If he makes some of his wild claims here in the Temple to the God-ordained authorities, we will be forced to arrest him and deal with him severely. If that does not work, we will go with the trap the Pharisees and Herodians have devised.

I lay awake into the third or possibly fourth watch of the night. Although I was physically exhausted, the different scenes of Jesus in the Temple paraded through my mind. I took the images and forced them to conform to our desires. When I finished the scene the way I wanted it, with Jesus losing support and crying out to us for help, I would try to sleep, but the scene flashed back with Jesus putting us to shame. The battle was fierce.

In the morning the battleground once again changed from my mind to the Temple courts. Jesus entered the Temple with his disciples and the early morning followers. Jesus' troops were plain and ordinary—the poor, fishermen, the people from the streets. The army of Caiaphas was resplendent with robes and turbans of finely colored cloth. Bulging purses hung from large sashes around larger bellies. Jesus was about to teach, but before he started, the procession of dignitaries marched to the place of battle.

The entire crowd became exceedingly quiet. The first thrust of battle was ours. "By what authority are you doing these things? And who gave you this authority?"

Jesus replied, "I will also ask you one question. If you answer me, I will tell you by what authority I am doing these things. John's baptism—where did it come from? Was it from heaven, or from men?"

We were taken aback and quickly huddled together. The people were waiting for our answer. If we said, "From heaven," he would ask us why we didn't believe John. If we said, "From men," the crowd would turn on us, since they thought John was a prophet. Instead of giving an answer, we said, "We don't know."

Jesus responded in kind. He didn't accept our excuse about not knowing, he just said, "Neither will I tell you by what authority I am doing these things." I felt frustration almost consume me. My jaws hurt from biting my own teeth. The first skirmish in the battle went to Jesus, but there was more to come.

As Jesus continued teaching the people with his stories, we went back to the meeting room. Everyone tried to talk at once. It wasn't intelligent conversation, it was questions recklessly hurled back and forth. "Why did we let him ask us that question? Why didn't we just say, 'We are the authorities here. You answer the question, and if we so decide, we will answer yours.'

Why didn't we prepare for this possibility?" The questions hurt and fanned our fury into even hotter flames. It was time for the tax issue.

We left the meeting room together, and quickly spread throughout the crowd to witness the next confrontation. I stationed myself where I could see and hear everything. I thought, "We are making the plans and setting the rules, but it almost seems like someone else is operating the plans and we are just being used." The feeling made me uncomfortable.

The Pharisees had gathered with some of their followers and some Herodians. Zerah, the most brilliant and persuasive man in Israel, was their spokesman. "Teacher," he said, "we know that you are a man of integrity and that you teach the way of God in accordance with the truth. You aren't swayed by men, because you pay no attention to who they are. Tell us then, what is your opinion? Is it right to pay taxes to Caesar or not?"

I crossed my arms over my chest and smiled. "This is it," I thought. "There is no way for him to get out of this. If he says to pay the taxes, we condemn him as one who goes against what Moses said. If he says to follow Moses, we run to the Romans, and they deal swiftly with anyone advocating not paying the taxes to Caesar. Let's see what you do now Rabbi from Galilee."

Again Jesus did not accept the question the way it was spoken. He seemed to know what was behind this and said, "You hypocrites, why are you trying to trap me? Show me the coin used for paying the tax."

One of the Herodians handed Zerah a denarius. Zerah offered it to Jesus, but he did not take it. Instead, Jesus pointed to the coin in Zerah's hand and said so that all could hear, "Whose graven image is this? And what does it say?"

I felt like someone kicked me in the stomach. Every Israelite knew the ten commandments. "You shall not make for yourselves any graven image . . . you shall not worship them." Our traditions had amplified this so that we could not even touch such a graven image. Yet here, in the Temple of God, our spokesman was holding the idol in his hand, while our enemy just pointed at it.

Also, we all knew what was on the denarius that Zerah was still holding: a graven image of Caesar, and an inscription that calls him divine as well as the highest priest and father of his country. The intensity was unbearable. Jesus was toying with us. Zerah's face was flushed and his heartbeat could be seen in the swollen veins of his neck. He said nothing, but someone in the crowd answered Jesus' question about whose graven image this was saying, "Caesar's."

Then, as if Jesus was graciously giving us a way out to pay taxes to Caesar, he said, "Give to Caesar what is Caesar's, and to God what is God's."

At this point we stepped aside to confer again and decided we would not ask any more questions or set up any confrontations in front of the people. He was too dangerous and crafty. We settled on the final plan of action. We would arrest him, but privately, away from the crowds. Then we would silence him forever.

As we discussed the logistics of arresting Jesus, Meraioth, one of the men employed by Caiaphas, said that one of Jesus' disciples had come to Caiaphas' home to ask about possible rewards for exposing Jesus' whereabouts. Immediately questions were multiplied. "Who was this disciple? Was he genuine? How did we know he was serious? Why would he want to do such a thing?"

Caiaphas was irritable and had suffered enough for today. He concluded our meeting with an order. "Malchus, investigate. If it's real, pay him thirty pieces of silver. That's all for today."

I wanted to pay him less money. Thirty pieces of silver was too much for this, but Caiaphas had clipped out these orders, and he was in no mood to be questioned. I picked up a bag of thirty pieces of silver from the steward of the treasury and went back out into the public courts of the temple with Meraioth.

"What are the arrangements?" I asked him. "Where are you to meet?"

Meraioth answered, "This disciple, Judas is his name, just said that he would get back in touch with me. He told me to tell the High Priest, that's all."

"Meraioth," I lectured him, "when you serve the High Priest you need to find out all the available information. Why? How? When? Where? Who? What will the problems be? How might Caiaphas be helped? What dangers are involved?" He bristled under my instructions.

The crowds were still surrounding Jesus, and Meraioth pointed out Judas. I dismissed him curtly with, "I'll take it from here."

Hanging around the crowds, I watched for an opportunity to speak with Judas without being noticed. When Jesus stopped teaching for a few minutes, people immediately began talking and questioning one another. I walked up to Judas and said, "I am your contact with the High Priest."

His eyes darted back and forth and he loudly whispered, "Not here, not here. I'll meet you tomorrow at sundown at the Pool of Bethesda." He turned and quickly walked away. But I wanted to check this out further and test him, so I walked with him.

He went away from the crowd and when we were somewhat isolated he looked at me with a mixture of terror and frustration. "I cannot be seen with you," he said. "Tomorrow at sundown I will meet you."

"Where are you staying at night?" I asked, ignoring his plight.

"We've been going to Bethany at night, but we'll probably stay here in Jerusalem after our Passover meal. Now leave me. Please," he added, almost begging.

I walked away with a clearer understanding of the person we were dealing with. I disliked him, did not trust him, and would rather have dealt with a viper. But, orders are orders, and this person might be the way of arresting Jesus.

My duties were finished for the day, and I did not want to go home. I left the Temple through the Dung Gate, and headed towards Caiaphas' house. Then, instead of heading west, I turned back north to a certain house where you could buy a few bowls of wine and have all the heated conversation you might desire. It was early afternoon, but I went there anyway and sat around with some merchants and various acquaintances. I didn't like this place, but there was nowhere else I wanted to be.

The next day I spent a few hours there again while waiting for sundown and the appointment with Judas. About sundown I headed for the Pool of Bethesda and milled around the crowds that were always there. This was a place of suffering and misery that I liked to avoid. Judas soon appeared and whispered, "Follow me."

I followed, but was unhappy to let him be in the lead. He went into the Temple and to one of the dark alcoves. He excitedly said, "Tomorrow night Jesus will be eating the Passover here in Jerusalem. I will meet you here at the Temple and lead you to him. Now, how much is this worth?"

I thought to myself, "He would settle for a lot less than thirty pieces of silver. I wish I could arrange the price with him, but orders are orders." "Here," I said. "Thirty pieces of silver." And I handed him the bag.

His expression changed. His features softened. He held the bag close to his face as if he would kiss the money. I thought, "Here it is! This is his God. This is his master, not the rabbi from Galilee."

I asked him, "Are you certain he will be alone?"

He answered, "There will be no more than a dozen or so. We will have to go very late—midnight or later."

"All right. But in the darkness and confusion, how can we be sure we get Jesus?"

Judas answered, "The one I greet with a kiss. That will be Jesus."

I wished there was another way. Talking with Judas there in the darkness was like bathing in sour wine. To think he would betray his teacher with a kiss almost moved me to pity Jesus, but I quickly banished any sympathy for my enemy. We finished all the details, and parted.

Now there was nothing for me to do but see that the guards were ready tomorrow night, and wait. Tell Caiaphas about the arrangements, and wait. Wait for our appointment with the traitor. Wait, and drink some more wine. Wait.

CHAPTER NINE

ROME

It is approaching dawn on this day before Caesar's birthday, and I realize I have not slept since awaking with the nightmare. Cleomus is near my cell and I ask him what happened to the prisoner who cracked. He says, "We made him sign the statement, 'Caesar is Lord,' and then turned him loose. He might be out of this prison, but he'll never get out of the one his fears have built."

"I think you're right," I respond. "I may be a prisoner in here, but I believe I am free in Jesus on my insides, and that's where I live."

"I've seen a lot of soldiers crack in battle, or just before a big battle," Cleomus continues. "Those men are worse than dead. They're dead while they still live."

"Cleomus, you have some real insights into life. You should be a teacher. You could help a lot of people by sharing with them the lessons you've learned."

The tough Roman guard looks at me with a strange hopeful gaze as if to ask, "Are you serious? Do you think I could ever amount to anything?"

"Cleomus my friend," I continue cautiously, realizing that I am sticking my neck out for this sword-wielding Roman, "I wish you were my brother in the Lord Jesus, except of course for being in prison. Then you could share about real freedom and life." He looks at me in stunned silence. I feel that he wants to talk, but he slowly and quietly turns and walks away.

I remember how I walked away from God. Even after Jesus touched me and the love and peace began to penetrate, I still resisted. My struggle lasted for seven weeks.

JERUSALEM

After the mob left that night with Jesus tied and in tow, I just stood there. I tried to think, but no thoughts came. I was in the shadows, and if anyone was still there, they either didn't notice me, or they didn't pay any attention.

I kept fingering my ear. I would have thought it was all a dream, except that the ring was gone. No doubt about it, my ear had been cut off, and replaced with the same one or a new one, but there was no longer a ring.

Before Jesus touched me, I was full of hate and murder. His touch had done something to all that. I felt no hatred, no animosity, no desire to stop his movement. A strange peace had taken hold of me, and I was just there, like a part of the background.

I realized some time later that I was heading toward Caiaphas' house. It was more like a mansion, a large beautiful building with a center courtyard. The family quarters were on the second floor. Only twice had I gone up there; both times Caiaphas was sick and he needed to give me some instructions.

On the ground floor a room opened onto the courtyard. It was large enough to accommodate the whole Sanhedrin. Of course this was not their official place of meeting, but I knew of several times they had gathered there.

A series of smaller rooms was also on the first floor. There was a private suite where Caiaphas met with various individuals or small groups. One of the rooms was my domain. Here I wrote instructions to subordinates, met with various persons, and carried out the duties given to me by Caiaphas. A window in my room overlooked both the courtyard and the large meeting room.

I don't remember getting there that night, but I came to the realization that I was in my room at Caiaphas' house watching the proceedings. I was surprised by a desire to know this Jesus, but he was being condemned, or actually was already condemned by the officials, and I just watched.

I also watched the group waiting in the courtyard. There was the one called Peter sitting near the fire with the servants and some of the mob. The peace and calm I had just experienced began to leave as I remembered Peter hitting me with the sword. I thought, "He was trying to kill me. He's a follower of Jesus, and he wanted to kill me, just like I wanted to kill Jesus."

Just then I heard Rachel, the girl in charge of the meeting room detail, say to Peter, "You're one of them, aren't you?" Peter denied it.

I felt betrayed. I was shocked that he said no. He had risked his life by striking me, and now he crumbled before this girl. In the meantime, Jesus was being insulted and spit on and set up for destruction. "I should follow someone like this?" I thought. "This is crazy. This is a dead cause."

Peter was being confronted again. I was agitated. Again he denied knowing Jesus. Then he cut loose with profane Galilean fisherman talk to try to prove he wasn't with Jesus. It was terrible. I wanted to see no more of this. "Malchus," I said to myself, "get yourself out of here!"

I went down an inside corridor to a private door on the outside wall. A haze of confusion kept my thoughts all muddled. I walked to my home in a stupor. Bethany and the children were sleeping.

I stood watching them, I don't know how long. Then I took a loaf of bread and tastelessly ate it chunk by chunk, as I walked back into the deserted streets. The heavy silence was broken by barking dogs warning me away from their houses. I don't remember where I walked, or for how long, but I found myself back again at the Mount of Olives. I sat against an old olive tree. If I slept, it was a dreamless murk. If I was awake, it was a mindless sitting.

The grey dawn began to lighten the eastern sky, and I was locked once again into the memory of my father taking me to the Temple as a young man. No matter how I tried to clear my head of the unpleasant memory, there it was: the priests, the lamb, the blood, the death.

I sat for hours. Thinking, yet not thinking, dozing, yet not sleeping. Remembering, but only the priests, the lamb, the blood and the death. About noon, darkness, heavy darkness came upon me.

The darkness was frightening. It wasn't clouds hiding the sun, although it was so dark I couldn't tell if there were clouds or not, but I don't think there were any before the darkness came.

With darkness came fear. In terror, I wept and cried out, "Have mercy Yahweh, have mercy!" The weeping continued, but I was up and walking again. In my wandering and weeping I wondered, "Where am I going? What's happening? Oh no! Am I going to Skull Hill? Lord Yahweh, I don't want to go to Skull Hill."

No matter how I pleaded and wept, my feet carried me to Skull Hill. Right above the Damascus road into the city where all could watch, on a hill that looked like a skull, the Romans crucified their victims. And of course, there was Jesus. Over his head was a sign, big enough for all those going along the road to read, "Jesus of Nazareth, King of the Jews."

"Caiaphas must be furious," I mused. I was glad to be out of his touch right then or I'd be the one scrambling around trying to get the sign changed. This was a mockery of Caiaphas and all the rulers of the Jews, not just that Pilate called him the King of the Jews, but it pointed out that he came from Nazareth. Supposedly nothing good could ever come from that place.

I was clearing away the fog in my brain, thinking about all the implications and intrigue, when suddenly I saw him. I mean, I had seen him before, but now, I really saw him.

He was naked. Not one shred of clothing was left on his body. "It's one thing for those Romans to kill and torture, but is this necessary?" I asked myself. "The humiliation and stripping of any worth or dignity? The ridicule and public shame?"

Then I saw the contortions of his body, the result of excruciating pain. I had seen hundreds of crucifixions, but I had never really thought about the agony of the person.

He was hanging from the cross. Huge spikes were driven into the base of his hands where enough bone could hold the weight of his body without tearing loose from the cross piece.

His feet were nailed to a slanted block of wood like a pedestal, and because of its angle, Jesus could not support his weight on his feet. If he wanted to talk, he had to pull up and lift the weight of his body with the spikes in his hands in order to get enough air in his lungs. "His hands probably don't feel the pain anymore because they're numb," I thought, "but the rest of his mutilated body must be right at the limit of feeling pain."

His back, or what had been Jesus' back, was visible as his head and shoulders hung forward. It was raw flesh that appeared to have no skin. If there was skin left on his back after the Romans scourged him, it was so torn, bruised and bloodied, that it no longer appeared as skin. The Roman who administered the scourging had used a whip with several thongs, each with a broken piece of bone at the end to rip and tear flesh and increase the pain. He had not shown mercy.

I moved closer. Jesus was wearing some kind of wreath like thing on his head. There were ugly thorns, sharp and nasty, sticking out of the wreath and into his flesh. I suddenly realized I was standing at the base of the cross. Blood was everywhere. Blood was all over his body. Blood was running down the cross. Blood was on the ground.

I was standing in blood! I turned to wretch and vomit. One of the Roman guards shoved me away and shouted to get out of there. As I stumbled away I noticed a crowd of women standing at a discreet distance, and there, I was certain, was Bethany.

I stumbled my way back to the city to a gathering place of sorts and bought a bowl of wine. Several acquaintances were there and began to ask, "Hey Malchus, where have you been? I haven't seen you since last night. Caiaphas wants to see you. It's really exciting, huh?" The questions continued, but I just gulped my bowl of wine and left.

Just outside the city gate I bought a skin of wine—not a small skin, a big one. I took the wine and headed right back to the Mount of Olives. It was still eerie and dark—yet I supposed, about midafternoon.

I drank the wine as fast as I could. There was only one goal in my mind—get drunk as fast as possible. As I slipped into unconsciousness, my last thoughts were of being shoved about by what looked like dead people in grave clothes coming out of the ground all around me.

* * *

The pounding in my head grew louder and harder. I opened my eyes to bright daylight and sharp pain. I was lying on the ground at the Mount of Olives. My clothes were covered with wine stains and dried vomit. Waves of nausea and aching undulated through my body. I staggered to my feet and headed for water.

It was broad daylight, but when I got to the nearest well, there was no one drawing water. "The Sabbath." I remembered then that it was the Sabbath. "Oh well, I must wash and get this burning thirst quenched." The first bucket of water went over my head. The second, down my throat.

I drank too much water, too fast. It made me feel worse, if that were possible. My stomach was quite upset, and the pounding in my head didn't cease. I headed for home and seclusion. People glared at me on the street. I thought they were thinking of me as a drunken bum—a sabbath breaker. A mother with two small children stepped back as I approached and shielded the children from me as if I was a criminal.

Bethany greeted me with red, swollen eyes, and an uninterrupted barrage of questions and words, "Oh, Malchus. Where have you been? Caiaphas is trying to find you. You look terrible. What happened? Oh, you smell terrible. Here, get your clothes off and lie down. I'll clean them up."

"It's all right, Bethany. It's the Sabbath, I think, and you don't need to clean up anything. I feel terrible. I just want to lie down."

I heard her a few times during the day telling the children that I would be all right. I was just a little sick, and not to bother me. I appreciated her consideration, especially as I could see she had been crying a lot. I would have been more understanding some other time. Right then, I had my own battle for survival.

I woke up before dawn on the first day of the week. I knew I had to get back and check in with Caiaphas, and although it was very early, I dragged myself from my pallet. I still felt terrible, but I had spent all the time in bed that I could tolerate. Quietly I washed and dressed and left for Caiaphas' house.

It was only a quick five minute walk, but I wandered around for over half an hour. Just before the sun came up, I heard distant thunder or perhaps a small earth tremor. I wasn't sure, but it didn't seem to be of significance and I went into my room. The table was full of messages from Caiaphas and others about what had been happening and what I should do.

Almost like an outsider, I read the notes, reports and instructions, and thought, "This is a real conspiracy. This is a closed issue before it was ever opened. I'm glad Pilate took a little of the victory away from us." I surprised myself by saying "us" and wondered if I was including myself again with the Jewish leaders.

Others began arriving in great haste. Four or five of the top leaders came and then even Annas and my father. I went to the meeting room to join them when Caiaphas came in. He was walking in his determined gait when he saw me. "Malchus, I've been trying ..."

The whole scene was interrupted by a troop of soldiers barging in and each trying to talk at the same time. These were Roman soldiers, and I didn't understand at first why they came here.

Annas took charge and commanded them to be quiet and to speak one at a time. These were the guards that had been posted at the tomb of Jesus to make sure no one would take away his body and start a rumor that Jesus had risen from the dead. They had even put a seal on the large stone. The emerging story was astonishing. Early that morning, a violent earthquake shook them from their feet. All agreed that brilliant light, like lightning, shone all about them. Some said they saw an angelic being in the light, others were too frightened to look. The seal was broken, the stone rolled away, and Jesus' body was no longer there. Some of the women who followed Jesus had come to the tomb at the same time and one guard said he heard the angel tell them that Jesus had risen from the dead. The others heard sound, but could not distinguish words.

The soldiers were led to a side room so the leaders could decide what to do. As soon as they were gone, everyone tried to speak at once and Annas again had to bring about order. He skillfully kept the issue focused on what directions to give the soldiers. "Doesn't anyone care what really happened at the tomb?" My mind burned with questions. "Was it really an angel? Did Jesus rise from the dead?" Rather, the issues were, how to deal with the guards; how much to pay them to lie and say the disciples came and stole the body of Jesus; and how to satisfy Pilate that the guards did their job.

I did not dare speak. My values and basic life direction were coming unraveled. I thought, "If there is an unforgivable sin it is surely to know the truth and still lie against it." Whatever happened at the tomb, of this I was certain: God had intervened. These men knew it was true. They heard the testimony of the guards whose lives were at risk for what happened. They knew the truth, they chose to lie. In the commotion of calling the soldiers back, paying them and telling them what to say, I quietly slipped away.

CHAPTER TEN

ROME

It is a bright sunny day, and I'm lying on my mat wide awake. Cleomus has gone off duty, yet I still think of him and his silent response to my words. After I pray for him, I want to hide, but there is nowhere to go. I want to hide from the cold reality that tomorrow is Caesar's birthday, but truth continues to assault me.

For the thousandth time, I mindlessly try counting the cracks in the ceiling, or the number of cockroaches visible from the mat. But even this kind of hiding is not allowable as my mind continues its relentless review.

For a little time I was able to hide from Bethany and Caiaphas and Jesus. It was so long ago, but it seems like only yesterday.

JERUSALEM

I went home and told Bethany about the meeting with Caiaphas and the soldiers. She listened in stunned silence, then suddenly brightened. She said, "Oh Malchus, it's true. He said he would rise from the dead, and he did. Oh, don't you see, he is the Messiah! He is the Messiah!"

I think I wanted to believe her, but the years of serving the tradition and the system caused me to resist. Perhaps I would have embraced Jesus, but Bethany, out of love and concern for me, began to press and push me to surrender my life to Jesus.

I'm not sure what she said, or how she said it, but I felt trapped and manipulated. I reacted with stupid anger and defensiveness. I don't know what I was defending, but it was as if I had to save my life. I said I was leaving for a few days and would see her when I got back. I took a few clothes and stalked out of the house like a pouting child.

Now where to go? From the experience of the last few days, I knew that if I just sat and thought, I would lose my mind. The forces fighting within me were tearing up my soul. There was a battle going on and I didn't seem to have much part in it. Something new was working to displace the old. I wanted to work with my hands, get dirty and sweat.

I then remembered the tanner. I had grown pretty close to Bartholomew during my apprenticeship, and had visited him about six months after going to work for Caiaphas. My intentions were to go out and see him regularly, but like so many of those intentions, it never came to pass. I did see him once a couple years later, but it had been many years now since I had gone out to the tanners.

The odor still hung in the air as I approached, but not as strong as I remembered. When I saw the buildings I wondered if Bartholomew was gone, or dead. Things were in a general state of disrepair. The gate was hanging loose, boards had fallen off some of the buildings, and the house had obviously been neglected for some time. An old hound dog greeted me with whining and whimpering. He looked like he was starving.

No one answered the door, so I opened it and went inside. Dust and filth covered everything, but there, lying on his cot was Bartholomew. He was emaciated. His eyes were big and glassy, sunken in two large hollows on his face. He managed a hint of a smile and gasped, "Malchus, Malchus."

The first job was to get some water in him and a little nourishment. I found enough to satisfy him, but as soon as he was resting better, I went and bought provisions. For the next ten days I nursed Bartholomew, made repairs on the house, and salvaged many of the hides. I worked sunup to sundown and slept the peaceful sleep of the exhausted. It was as though the turmoil and torment were moved far enough back that they left me alone for those days.

I returned home to a mixed reception. Bethany was relieved to see me, and so were the children, but they were obviously angry and didn't know how to deal with me. When I explained to them where I had been, they were a little more understanding, but we weren't a united family yet.

* * *

Two weeks had passed since the day we arrested Jesus. I did not want to see Caiaphas—ever again—but I knew I must. Considering our bond-slave relationship, this length of time out of contact was inexcusable. He would have heard about Peter hitting me with a sword, but no one really knew the details. Had I reported back in a day or two he would have been angry, reprimanded me and restored me to his service. Now I knew I would get a cold, formal reception as an outsider.

When I got to his house I went to the room assigned to me. The room was bare. All my things were gone. I went to Caiaphas' rooms and walked in. Meraioth, now his secretary, said, "Hello Malchus. I'll see if Caiaphas will see you." He went into the inner room and simply left me standing.

After several minutes he returned and said, "Please be seated. Caiaphas will see you shortly." With that he went back to the inner room, and left me alone. I used to give him directions, and now, two weeks later he keeps me waiting like a nobody. Oh well, I had expected this.

I waited at least a half hour. Finally Meraioth came back and said, "Caiaphas will see you now."

I walked up to his table. He did not get up or greet me. I was left standing there in an uncomfortable silence. Finally I said, "Caiaphas, I don't know what to say."

He quickly answered, "I do Malchus. Where is the ring?"

"When we arrested Jesus, I . . ."

Caiaphas interrupted with, "Please do not refer to him by that name. You may call him the Nazarene, or whatever, but do not use his name."

I answered again, "When we arrested the uh, Nazarene, I was leading the group. When we got to him I had a club swinging over my head to level him, then his follower Peter hit me with a sword. He cut off my ear, then Jesus, the Nazarene, touched my head: the ear was back, but the ring was gone."

Caiaphas glared at me. "Malchus," he said, "I've had all of that Galilean rabbi I want. I needed you and you were gone. I could still use you, but quite frankly, I don't trust you right now. Get out of here and get your thinking straightened out. When you come to your senses, I'll see if I can find a place for you, but I don't want to see you again until this is settled. If it weren't for your father, and for your past service, I'd have you beaten."

* * *

During those next few weeks I continued to go to Bartholomew's daily. Sometimes I spent the night, but a routine began again in our home. I took Jehoiada with me a few times, and he seemed to like the work once he got over the problem of the odor. We were like a family, yet there was still a division needing to be healed. The battle continued in my soul, and I felt like a victim instead of a participant.

Although Bartholomew responded to the care I gave, he was a very sick man, and was obviously going to die. Bethany suggested I bring him to our home where she could look after him. This pleased me more than I could say. I was touched by her compassion and willingness to serve this man she knew only from my reports of him.

Bartholomew had a cart for hauling skins which I had left out in the sun and air to "freshen up" for the journey to our house. Bethany and Sarah joined Jehoiada and me for the big event. We hired a donkey to pull the cart and the children loved the trip to Bartholomew's on the donkey's back. It was hard to walk along side holding Jehoiada and Sarah, but their delight made it bearable. It was also the most togetherness Bethany and I had experienced for a long time.

Arriving at Bartholomew's, Jehoiada took Bethany's hand and literally pulled her into the house while I brought up the rear with Sarah. He led her to the bed where Bartholomew's saucer like eyes revealed his nervousness. "See, see Mommy," he excitedly cried, "he's a nice man. I told you he was a nice man, Mommy."

An instant bond was formed and without introduction or formality of any kind, Bethany took the jar of urine and emptied it outside. She brought water and began to wash his face and hands without giving him an opportunity to protest her ministrations. She was incredible. "My husband and my son have told me about you, and I am happy to meet you at last. You are to me as a brother of my father or mother, and I will be pleased for you to come and stay in our home," she said.

She was so tender that Bartholomew's natural shyness was dispelled, and yet so firm and resolute that his protests were not even voiced. She guarded his dignity with her life's pattern of respect, and quickly and naturally wiped his tears as she lovingly held his head and continued her washing and stroking.

Jehoiada and I hitched the donkey to the wagon, and spread as many well cured skins as we could find over the wood. I noticed him smoothing and patting the make shift bed. When I went inside and picked up Bartholomew I was shocked at how little he weighed. It was like picking up a child.

"Be careful, Malchus," Bethany ordered. Strangely, I felt no resentment or anger as I had for years whenever she offered advice or gave direction. I smiled at my friend, who was giving silent assent to the hard reality that we were taking control over his life. He surely died some as he yielded himself to the care of others. It may have been easier because it was loving care, but it was still a part of dying that we all naturally hate and fight.

Bethany rode with Bartholomew on the cart, and tried to comfort him and ease his suffering. My thoughts of her tenderness were soon replaced by annoyance, then anger at her constant carping. When the donkey would surge, she would say, "Malchus, be more careful!" When we hit a bump or a rut she would just say my name, "Malchus." Even though it was only my name that was spoken, I heard in my heart, "You clumsy oaf. Look out where you're going. Don't you care? This is all your fault."

I tried hard to make the journey as smooth as possible, and I took each complaint personally as if it were an attack on me. By the time we arrived home, I was furious. I carried

Bartholomew into the house and placed him on the bed we had fixed in our center room. I unhitched the donkey, put the cart at the side of our house, and went to return the animal. I was so glad to get out of the house and away from Bethany, I don't think I even said where I was going.

I had done business with the owner of the donkey before. Several times I had hired animals from him, and had always been pleased with the arrangements. This time he was different. Early that morning he had been nice and pleasant and when I asked about a deposit he said, "I know you Malchus. It's not necessary. We'll just settle up when you bring the donkey back."

Now he was like a different man. He demanded payment which I thought double the rate. He complained about the condition of the donkey, and spoke to me with shouts that others could hear. I was still angry from the trip and flashed back at him with anger, "You're trying to cheat me. That's at least twice the amount the donkey's worth. What do you take me for, a fool?"

He responded, "Just who do you think you are? You can't come in here and get just what you want thinking you're some kind of important person. Who do you think you are anyway?" Picking up a shoveling fork and glaring at me, he acted as if I was mad enough to strike him.

He was right. I was angry enough to hit him, but by then a crowd had gathered and I noticed some temple guards. Someone had been talking to this man, and I was set up. I was smart enough to pay him, or rather throw the money at his feet, and shout, "Here, here are two farthings for one donkey for one day." I turned quickly and walked away, feeling something like Bartholomew—like control over my life had been taken away from me. Oh well, a live dog is better than a dead lion, and I felt like a dog, kicked around by Bethany, by this donkey tender, by Caiaphas and his blasted guards, and yes, even kicked around by God.

Bethany met me at the door. "O Malchus, Malchus, he's dying. He's out of his mind. What can we do? What can we do?"

Bartholomew was feverish and sweating. He tossed his frail body about on the bed like a dried leaf in the wind. I said, "Get some towels and keep him as dry as possible so he doesn't get a chill. He wasn't up to the trip, but hopefully this is a reaction he can survive."

Bethany was constantly calling on God for Bartholomew, and as she toweled his feverish body she suddenly stopped, looked at me and entreated, "Malchus, will you please pray for him?" Her request was so genuine and sincere that I automatically began. "Lord," I prayed and then stopped with the startling realization that He was God far away, and not near as I had always assumed. "Lord," I started again, "come and bless Bartholomew and spare his life for a time." Silently I added, "and draw me unto yourself."

CHAPTER ELEVEN

ROME

A different mood prevails among us here in prison on this day before Caesar's birthday. The usual positive attitudes and encouragement are missing. Somberness has engulfed us like a cloud, and I want private space, available only in my heart and mind. We're in this together, and we understand one another.

One more cycle of the sun around the earth and this phase of my life will be over. Either I will be outside the Kingdom of God with a cowardly confession that Caesar is Lord, or I will be preparing to die in some horrible way. These bars and walls will no longer hold me. Ropes or nails or arena walls will hold me, while godless men destroy my body.

I pray, "Lord, I'm yours. My life and all I am and have belong to you. Whatever you want to do, I accept. If this dying, being killed for you, is what you want, then I'm . . . Oh, Lord, help my unwillingness. If you allow this, help me die in a way that honors you, but Jesus, I am so frightened. Come Lord and quiet this child's heart, and my brothers' and sisters' too."

JERUSALEM

After I had prayed for Bartholomew, he fell into a restful sleep. I was shocked at the apparent connection between my prayer and his relief. I was thinking about it, and also wondering why Bethany just took it for granted. I considered the possibility that if God heard my prayer about Bartholomew, he might also draw me unto himself. I wasn't sure how I felt about that, but it was in God's hands now, not mine.

It was now less than a week until Pentecost, and I spent most of the time around the house. There was the water damage on the back corner of the house, and the rock garden Bethany wanted me to arrange, and the pair of sandals Jehoiada wanted to make with me, and the branches of the nut tree behind our house that was perfect for a swing, and, of course, there was Bartholomew.

As I fixed things and busied myself around the house, I often overheard Bethany talking to Bartholomew. I liked to listen to her tell of the times she heard Jesus teaching in the Temple, or explain the stories he told. When she told Bartholomew, I felt free to listen and absorb the truths, but any time she spoke to me about Jesus and his teachings, I felt attacked and challenged by my wife.

One day I was making a pair of sandals in the main room while Bethany was feeding Bartholomew. She spoke lovingly to him as she put the very small portions of food in his mouth. He motioned with a hand and spoke in his feeble voice, "That's enough. Thank you," and then he fell asleep.

Bethany remained there by his side, and soon began praying. She was stroking his head and talking to God about him. She thanked God for bringing Bartholomew to us, and all that he was. She thanked him for what it had done for us as a family and especially for the children. She talked on about her happiness in serving Bartholomew, and then she began to discuss his various needs and problems: his inability to take enough nourishment; the considerable pain in his back and the sores where the little weight of his frail body press on the mat; and the difficulty he had coughing and clearing his throat.

Bethany's prayer drew me like a magnet. I was across the room working on the sandals, but as she prayed, I came over and stood just behind her. She went on for some time in this intimate conversation with God about Bartholomew, and then stopped and looked at me, a little surprised that I was there. As she looked at me with an expression that questioned my presence, I smiled, put my hand on her shoulder, patted her and said, "Amen." She put her hand on my hand and I stood there with her. I left after a few moments because I didn't want Bethany to see my tears.

On Friday, the day of preparation, I heard a loud knock on our door followed by Bethany's shrieks of delight, "Abba, Abba!" This time the presence of the man of God with the silver shock of hair did not upset me. I was genuinely glad to see Asaph.

"Welcome Asaph," I said as I embraced my father-in-law. He wanted very much to question me, but the delighted screams of Jehoiada and Sarah, and the presence of Bartholomew took precedence. After Bethany finally pried the children off beloved "Abbasaph," he was introduced to Bartholomew.

As naturally as talking or breathing, Asaph placed his hand upon Bartholomew and blessed him. Then, with his hand still on Bartholomew's head, he raised his other hand to God, lifted his eyes and blessed God for Bartholomew and our family. Asaph's presence was like a warm fire on a chilly day.

Since it was late afternoon on Friday we all hurried to be ready for Sabbath by sundown. The table was prepared in the main room, Bethany was cooking and cleaning, I cleaned up Bartholomew and got him propped up, Asaph took his traveling bag into the room with Jehoiada where he would stay. We all scurried around and washed and dressed, and just at sundown we gathered around the sabbath table.

Placing her shawl over her head, Bethany ushered in the Sabbath with, "Blessed are you O Lord our God, who has commanded us to kindle the Sabbath lights." She lit the candles and the light of the flame mixed with the light of hope and joy set apart from all other peoples. "Bless Sarah that she would be like Rachel and Leah . . . Bless Jehoiada that he would be like Ephraim and Manasseh."

Lifting the bread I blessed it as had my father, and his father and his father's father, "Blessed are you O Lord our God, King of the Universe, who brings forth bread from the earth." And lifting the cup, "Blessed are you O Lord our God, King of the Universe, who brings forth the fruit of the vine." And because it was the Sabbath before the Feast, "Blessed are you O Lord our God, King of the Universe, who has kept us in life and enabled us to reach this day."

What a happy meal. The children excitedly telling Asaph every detail of their young lives and adventures, and this grand old man of God listening with interest and rapt attention. Bartholomew experiencing family again after so many years, myself with a particle of hope for a full life again with Bethany, and Bethany with her ongoing depth of faith, godliness and contentment.

After the meal, Asaph stood up and blessed us. He lifted his hands and said, "Lord God of Abraham and Isaac and Jacob, giver of life and all good things, who rested from your labors on the seventh day, who had created us on the sixth day to begin lives by resting with you on the Sabbath day, we bless you and thank you. Thank you for separating us by the light of the Sabbath. Thank you that your light shines in this home and on these people. Thank you for the coming Feast—may we feast on your goodness in your presence forever. May you always bless us and keep us. May your face always shine upon us with favor and love. May your hope and expectation be fulfilled in us and may we always walk in your peace. Amen."

We all echoed, "Amen," and before long were bedded down for the night.

The following day we rested as usual. Asaph and I had our time together, in fact we talked for many hours. I told him everything that had happened to me since the arrest of Jesus. I felt a tremendous weight being lifted off my shoulders in just sharing it all with another person, especially one so gracious and understanding as Asaph.

After I finished my story, he smiled and nodded his head. Then he began to question me about everything I could remember from the time of the crucifixion until I left Caiaphas' on Sunday morning. He was truly excited about the possibility of Jesus rising from the dead, but was just not sure about it. He said, "If this is true, Malchus, may he show me—may he show us."

Then we talked on about my future, or really my lack of future with Caiaphas. I told him that no matter what, I could not go back because of the lies and intrigue that took place seven weeks before. I was in the terrible predicament of being bound by oath to serve Caiaphas for life, but the ring was cut off of my ear, and my conscience would no longer allow me to serve him.

Caiaphas could put me in prison, confiscate our property, take my life without a trial, and even sell Bethany, Jehoiada and Sarah into slavery. Asaph's concern gave me some comfort, but I wondered what Caiaphas would do when he decided I've had time to come to my senses?

On Sunday morning Asaph and I went to the Temple for the presentation of the loaves. Bethany stayed home since the children were still sleeping and Bartholomew needed her care. It was good to be with Asaph. He was serious, but very pleasant company. He did not make me feel on edge like so many other serious people did.

An unusually large number of visitors were in Jerusalem for the Feast of Pentecost, and the Temple was crowded. After the waving of the loaves we were swept out together with the crowd—such a large mass of people were moving at once there was no way to resist the flow of bodies. We had entered through the Dung Gate, and were leaving by the Zion Gate.

A few cubits outside the gate, the crowd was beginning to disperse when a blast of sound stopped us all. It was a calm day with no clouds, yet the sound was like a violent wind in a terrible storm. We hurried toward the sound, as did many, and there we saw a large house with some of the followers of Jesus staggering out into the street like drunken men. They were praising God, and shouting, lifting their hands in prayer, and jabbering strange sounds.

I heard people muttering, "Look at those disgusting people—drunk at this hour of the day." "They're praising God in my native tongue," I heard some foreigners exclaim. Some took hold of those speaking and asked, "How did you learn Elamese?" Or, "Were you raised in Egypt?" But these were all Galileans, and they didn't answer the questions, they just kept speaking in the various languages.

Then Peter stood up and motioned for attention. My stomach began to churn and spasm. He said the men were not drunk, it was only the third hour, but that what we were experiencing was the fulfillment of the words of the prophet Joel, "In the last days,God says, I will pour out my Spirit on all people. Your sons and daughters will prophesy, your young men will see visions, your old men will dream dreams. Even on my servants, both men and women, I will pour out my Spirit in those days, and they will prophesy."

Peter went on about Jesus and his miracles and said, "This man was handed over to you by God's set purpose and fore-knowledge; and you, with the help of wicked men, put him to death by nailing him to the cross. But God raised him from the dead, freeing him from the agony of death, because it was impossible for death to keep its hold on him."

Those words felt like hammer blows in my mind, in my stomach, throughout my whole being. Peter went on, but I was mesmerized by the vision of the arrest of Jesus, the healing of my ear, and then the time at Caiaphas' when the soldiers brought their report. I felt terrible. I had been a significant part of the fight against God. I had chosen to be an enemy of God and of His Christ.

In my grief and remorse I was somehow brought back in touch with the surroundings, and obviously many others were convicted also. Men began asking, "What shall we do? What shall we do?"

Peter answered, "Repent and be baptized, every one of you, in the name of Jesus Christ so that your sins will be forgiven. And you will receive the gift of the Holy Spirit. The promise is for you and your children and for all who are far off—for all whom the Lord our God will call."

Peter was saying more, but I was set. I acknowledged that Jesus, whom I had crucified, was the Messiah and in a new way turned my life over to God. I wanted baptism and cleansing. I wanted to be reconciled with this Jesus more than I had ever wanted anything in all my life.

Peter gave some instructions about baptism, and many of us went to the designated location. Only then did I realize Asaph was still with me, and that he too was going to be baptized. We smiled at one another, put our arms around each other and walked on.

When the baptizing started, I realized there were thousands of us, and about a hundred people doing the baptizing. As God would have it, both Asaph and I wound up in a group of about thirty led by Peter. Together we confessed our sins and our desire for a new life in Jesus the Christ of God. Peter gave a short teaching about dying to the world in the water of baptism that is connected somehow to Jesus' death, and then rising again with Jesus when he rose from the dead as we come out of the water.

We were in a shallow pool, and Peter had us sit in the water; as our turn for baptism came, he would lay us back into the water. When it was my turn, he looked intently at me trying, I was sure, to remember who I was and how he knew me.

I chuckled to myself at his quandary, but quickly came back to the baptizing at hand as a warm presence of what I would describe as liquid love, was poured through me. This sensation, different from any other feeling I had known, went throughout my entire body. I got up from the water filled with joy, and stumbled out of the pool as if I were drunk.

I laughed, and laughed, and raised my hands in prayer and laughed between "Thank You's" to God. I thought I was still saying "Thank You's," but I heard myself speaking unintelligible sounds. They sounded like gibberish, but they expressed my gratitude for the liquid love in a way that I couldn't do by thinking about it.

Asaph was experiencing the same thing. I looked at him, heard him, and laughed. He laughed, then Peter joined us, also making these strange sounds and quickly being infected with the laughter that possessed Asaph and me. He laughed and spoke nonsense with us for a few moments, then went off with some of the others.

I wanted to go home and share with Bethany, but couldn't speak it. I looked at Asaph and he seemed to understand, so again arm in arm, laughing and gibbering we staggered towards home.

People stared at us, and at the other groups of. . . whatever we were, and glared. One very religious woman stood before us, blocking our path. She snarled, "Drunk. And on a High Feast Day." Turning to Asaph she snarled, "And you, a priest."

We roared with laughter and she was enraged. We stumbled away, before she could hit us with a stick she had in hand. I was certain she thought she would be serving God by chastising us any way she could.

We staggered on toward our destination. Instead of letting up, the laughter and gibbering even intensified as we approached the house. The door was open, and the family could be seen as we came up the path. "Now what?" I thought to myself. "What will this be like with the family?"

CHAPTER TWELVE

JERUSALEM

We got home, but I'm not sure how. Asaph and I could be heard laughing from a distance and when we burst into the room, Bethany, Jehoiada, Sarah and Bartholomew all greeted us with round eyes, mouths agape and stunned silence.

"Let me tell you what happened," I started to say, and then laughed. There was no fighting this laughter, and I completely surrendered. Asaph had to sit down. He held his stomach, now sore from laughing, but he didn't stop. He began new and fresh.

Bethany shook her head, but she smiled. Then a little chuckle sneaked out of her mouth, Sarah gave a "tee hee," and Jehoiada a "huh." Asaph and I responded to their beginnings of laughter with shrieks and howls. Now there was no stopping any of us. Even Bartholomew caught the holy joy with laughter, and his frail body shook.

Before long Asaph and I collapsed from exhaustion and just sat on the floor, watching this beautiful family. No wonder so many people thought we were drunk earlier. My wife and children and even sick old Bartholomew looked and acted like they were drunk. They were definitely intoxicated, but the spirit that filled them was from a new wine, not just fermented, but empowered by God—the wine of God's own presence within.

Soon Jehoiada fell on Asaph's lap, and I pulled Sarah to me, followed by Bethany. The laughter finally subsided, and we sat there on the floor of our main room with Bartholomew. Asaph and I shared the telling of what happened from the time we left the Temple until we staggered through our door. Bethany was delighted and kept saying, "Thank you, Lord. Thank. you, Lord."

Bartholomew asked, "Malchus, could I be baptized too?"

"Well, yes. I think so. I, uh, I don't know why not, uh, who would do it though?" I stumbled and stammered.

"I had hoped you would Malchus, and maybe you sir," he said addressing Asaph, "could help in it?"

Asaph quickly said, "Absolutely! Malchus, you shall baptize your friend, and I will assist you."

Since Bartholomew couldn't be moved or put into water, we thought it would be fine with the Lord to just pour some water over his head. Bethany got a cloth to soak up the water, and Asaph held his head and prayed. It was a beautiful prayer, and then he looked at me and said, "Go ahead, Malchus."

I had been told that Jesus had said to make disciples of everyone, baptizing them in the name of the Father, Son and Holy Spirit, and I had heard Peter say earlier in the day to be baptized into the name of Jesus. I wasn't sure what to say and I didn't remember the words Peter said when he baptized me, so I said, "Bartholomew, as a servant of Jesus the Messiah, by his authority and into his name I baptize you in the name of the Father and the Son and the Holy Spirit."

I was worried about what I said, and how I said it, but God evidently wasn't so concerned, because it worked. Bartholomew began speaking in the same unintelligible way we did. The sounds weren't loud, and it didn't go on very long, but it was the same. Then, as Asaph and I joined Bartholomew in the strange speaking, Bethany joined with us also.

Asaph stayed with us for a few wonderful days. Daily in the Temple we listened to the apostles teach. Sometimes Bethany came with us, but when she didn't, we repeated everything once we returned home. With joy in the Lord, and sadness at parting we said good-bye to our beloved father and now brother in the Lord. We also had to say good-bye to Bartholomew.

I went to the Temple alone that day and heard Peter telling about the time Jesus called him to be a disciple and a fisher for men. It was so humorous to hear Peter tell about his doubts and gruffness and muttering, and then his amazement when he realized a miracle was taking place and his boat was swamped with fish. I was excited about sharing this with my family and was hoping I could be funny too.

After the evening meal we were all seated in our main room where Bartholomew's mat had been arranged. We sang from the Psalms, "Create in me a pure heart, O God, and renew a steadfast spirit within me. Cast me not away from Your presence, and take not your Holy Spirit from me." Bartholomew's lips were moving with us, but he was so weak you could not hear him unless you put your ear right at his mouth.

I prayed, but it didn't seem so much like prayer anymore. It was now a family conversing with our Father God. I thanked him for Jesus and his blood and his resurrection. I thanked him that we were his family too, and that Jesus was here with us by his Spirit. I thanked him for the apostles and the other followers of the Way. I thanked him for whatever came to mind until Jehoiada spoke out, "Good-bye Bartholomew."

I glanced at my son, bravely trying to smile, but the tears were already spilling from his eyes. Then I looked at Bartholomew, or rather the discarded body where Bartholomew used to live. There was an expression of great peace and relief on this beloved face that had masked over such pain these past weeks.

We all cried. There was a mixture of gratitude that he was no longer suffering, but plenty of sorrow at saying good-bye to this man we had all come to love and accept into our family, even in his sickness. He was a part of us, and we would miss him.

"Bethany, you prepare the body for burial, and Jehoiada and I will go and prepare the grave," I directed.

"Yes, my Lord Malchus," she responded with a purity and respect that melted my heart. Tears were flowing like streams down my cheeks, but I was not sure of the cause— Bartholomew's death? Or the unity of my family? Or the loving submission of my wife? Most likely it was all of these reasons.

Jehoiada and I took a lamp into the yard and I dug a grave for my friend. I was grateful that the ground was soft from recent rains, and I knew just where the grave should be. We had picked a spot for planting a pomegranate tree that Bethany had been growing from seed. I thought this would be very appropriate. It felt good to sweat as I prepared the resting place.

When the grave was finished, I carried out the body, now wrapped in a clean cloth for burial. As the family gathered around I laid him tenderly in the earth, and said, "Dust to dust, ashes to ashes. We plant the body of our brother Bartholomew in the earth from which he came, as we wait for the resurrection of his body when our Lord Jesus comes again and calls all those who died in him back to life—eternal life."

Jehoiada interrupted my service with, "Abba, when Jesus comes back and makes Bartholomew alive again will he still be sick, or can he go on walks with me and eat some of Momma's cakes?"

"When Jesus makes him alive again, Jehoiada," I answered, "Bartholomew will go on walks with you and eat Momma's cakes."

"Oh good," Jehoiada said. "I hope Jesus hurries up."

"Me too," I said, and so did Bethany, and even Sarah put in her, "Me too."

After covering the body, I planted the seedling pomegranate tree over the grave. I said, "Just like the seed that grew into this little tree will grow into a bigger tree filled with fruit, so Jesus will raise up the body of our friend Bartholomew. Lord Jesus, like Jehoiada said, 'Please hurry up,' and thank you for letting us know and love your friend Bartholomew. Amen."

The family responded with, "Amen. Yes Jesus." And another, "Please hurry up, Jesus."

* * *

Asaph had been concerned about our safety since Caiaphas was certainly aware by now of our defection to become "Followers of the Way" as we were now known. Before he left, he told Peter and John about my problem and a few days later they asked to meet with me at the home of Joanna.

I shared with them the situation about being Caiaphas' bond-slave and how that could mean my life, and the family being sent to jail or sold into slavery. I also filled them in as much as possible on Caiaphas' frustrations and the way he thought and acted.

We discussed this for about an hour, and since nothing definite was taking shape, I was told to sleep on it and pray, and try to find the mind of the Lord for the situation. They also promised to pray about it with all the apostles, and consider again tomorrow.

After John left, Peter and I were alone. I had never been alone with him before and I began to be irritable. I didn't know why, but a growing edginess crept into or out of my soul.

Peter went to the water jar and helped himself to a drink. His actions irritated me and I felt anger toward him. He asked, "Would you like a drink, Malchus?"

"No," I answered, with my feelings seeping into my voice.

"What's the matter, Malchus?" My irritation was obvious even to this blustering apostle.

I lied and said, "Oh nothing."

"Come on, Malchus. Something's eating at you. What is it?"

I realized that this man who would try to walk on water wouldn't let go once he set his sights on something. I let some of the oozing anger out with, "Well, you know, it's like when you come in here you just sort of take over. This is Joanna's house, yet you just help yourself to the water as if you owned the place."

Peter responded with, "Don't be cowardly, Malchus, and don't be petty. All I am and have belongs to the community. And Joanna's water is God's water. It all belongs to Him, and she said she gave everything to the Lord and to his people. It's something more isn't it?"

I answered slowly since I knew I was on shaky ground. "I don't know Peter, but when I'm around you it seems like you take up all the space. You fill up the room with your presence and I feel like there's no room for me."

Peter bluntly threw it back in my face. "Malchus, don't try to put your feelings on me. If you have a problem say so, but don't make me into some kind of monster. I walk into a room like anybody else. I have no more power or control over you than you give me."

I backed down in the presence of his intensity and the truth he was expressing. I whimpered, "I don't know Peter."

"Don't whine," Peter demanded. "I hate whining, and it's not right for a follower of the Way to be a whiner. It's a mark of unbelief." Now he seemed angry too.

I stood looking at this rugged fisherman. In the quiet the Lord must have pricked Peter's memory for he abruptly changed his demeanor and almost whispered, "Oh Malchus, I'm sorry. We've never cleared up the sword in the garden have we? I'm sorry I hit you, and I ask your forgiveness."

Tears filled my eyes and spilled down my face. I tried to stay in control, but they flowed as if a dam had burst. I said nothing.

Peter pressed on asking me to forgive him, but I withheld my mercy. He grew silent and just looked at me. The tears continued to flow but I avoided his eyes. Then as if the tears had washed away an unseen barrier I stammered, "It's not the sword, Peter. I followed soon after to Caiaphas' house. I watched, wanting to believe, wanting to trust, wanting something to hold on to." I stopped talking for the crying. Peter was stunned. I continued, "At the fire I heard you deny Jesus. I heard you curse and swear and call down an oath that you weren't a follower. You were the brave hero who was going to defend Jesus in the garden, and I respected that, but I couldn't handle the denial. It was too much."

Now tears were spilling from Peter's eyes and he cried, "Oh Malchus, I'm sorry. It wasn't just Jesus I sinned against, it was you too. I am sorry," he sobbed, "please forgive me."

Through my tears I mumbled, "It's okay, Peter."

He replied, "No, it's not okay. Please forgive me."

"It doesn't matter any more, Peter."

With great sorrow, and intensity, sobbing, and grief, Peter took my face in his hands so I had to look through his watering eyes into his hurting soul. "For God's sake, Malchus, forgive me," he cried. "For Jesus sake, forgive me for that sin."

"Yes," I replied.

"Say it," he roared. "Say you forgive me in Jesus name."

I slowly lifted my arms and put them around him. Each word was spaced with a sob, "I forgive you Peter, in Jesus name."

For a long time we wept in an embrace. I experienced the same sensation as when I surrendered to Jesus, although it was different, somehow. A huge stone was washed away by the tears and Peter's embrace. A new peace filled me. It was peace from Jesus. It was peace with Peter. It was a peace with Father. It was also peace with myself.

I was grateful for the peace, and I suspected I would need it. I was right.

CHAPTER THIRTEEN

ROME

The bag of leather working tools is still in my cell, and I begin to repair Cleomus' sandals that are now mine. It feels good to work the needle and repair the strap. I wish there was some leather in the bag and I could work on some other sandals. Just as I finish one of the guards shouts at me, "What are you doing?"

"I've just finished repairing Cleomus' sandals. Or actually they're mine now, since he took mine." I think Cleomus might look bad leaving the tools with me, so I try to make it sound like he confiscated my sandals. It is interesting to me that I am looking at Cleomus as an ally against this guard.

Grabbing the bag out of my hand, the guard looks through the tools. "I'll leave this for Cleomus and see if your story checks out," he growls. "Cleomus should have known better than to leave it here with you, and you should have known better than to keep it. You have no business here with something like this."

He takes out the awl I use for punching leather. "Stick out your hand," he orders. I shudder and put out my left hand. "No, the other one," he demands. As soon as my right hand is extended, he jams the awl through the palm of my hand, punching out a small channel of flesh from front to back.

In spite of my efforts, a sharp spasm of pain evokes a near silent grunt from me. My teeth are clenched, and the way I took his cruelty seems to impress him. He nods his approval, but then says, "You'd better get used to pain, Christian." He laughs as he saunters off swinging my bag in the air.

JERUSALEM

Those days following Pentecost could have been ominous and frightening. Caiaphas could sell me and my whole family into slavery, confiscate all of our property, or do whatever his enraged mind desired. Yet when the Holy Spirit was poured out upon us, we received a measure of happiness and peace that even the dark cloud of Caiaphas could not take away. Even Bartholomew's death was a peace filled happening. I grew closer to Peter after our time of washing the uncleanness in me, and also lifting a little of the burden he will always carry from his denial of Jesus.

Peter told me late one day that the apostles had met and prayed much about our family, and had finally sensed some direction. I was to meet with him and John and maybe James the brother of the Lord on the following afternoon.

The day began as usual. I was up earlier than the rest of the family and spent some time reading from our scroll of Isaiah. As I talked with the Lord and sought his mind and direction, I felt an excitement and expectation, but also a seriousness and need to be ready for anything.

After Bethany and the children awoke, we ate together and spent time praying and thanking God for his great love. We then gathered at the Temple where groups of Followers of the Way were teaching and sharing together. The apostles were together somewhere else that morning, but there was no lack of teachers and leaders.

The children loved these times—playing with other children and listening to the stories. Sometimes the children would wander from group to group until they found an excited story teller, then they would sit and listen. There were favorite teachers, but we didn't refer to them as teachers. They were brothers or sisters in the Lord.

About noon, together with three or four others, we went to our neighbor's home for a common meal. The desire to be together was so strong that if guests were not at our house for a meal, we were at someone else's. One of the brothers was in need, and I began making a pair of sandals for him, and also gave him some money. My stash of treasure was shrinking, but there was still an ample supply.

At the time of prayer, about three in the afternoon, we went back to the Temple to hear more teaching, to be with our new brothers and sisters, and especially to hear from Peter and John the word from the apostles about our situation with Caiaphas. As we entered the gate called Beautiful, we looked back and saw Peter and John coming. Waving and stopping to wait for them, we watched an incredible miracle.

The beggar was being carried to his place near the gate where he had begged daily for many years. He had been crippled from birth and was well known by everyone in Jerusalem simply as, the beggar. He had just been put down when Peter and John were about to pass by. He must have asked them for money because they stopped, and there was some conversation. We were too far away to hear what was said, but soon Peter reached down and took the beggar by the hand and stood him up on his feet.

He seemed a little shaky at first, but soon walked about, then ran about, and then began jumping about. He ran into the Temple, jumping and praising God. People recognized the beggar, the cripple who had sat by the Gate Beautiful, and they were amazed. The Followers of the Way joined in the praise and celebrating, and a huge crowd gathered to see what was going on.

Of course Peter began to preach. He started off with, "Men of Israel, why does this surprise you? Why do you stare at us as if by our own power and godliness we had made this man walk?" Then he went on about the power of the name of Jesus, and how God raised Jesus from the dead. He said that they crucified Jesus out of ignorance, and they should repent and turn to God to be cleansed of their sins and be refreshed from the Messiah, even Jesus.

As they preached I noticed the temple guards, some priests and a group of Sadducees, some spreading out through the crowd and others making their way to Peter and John. There was a sinking feeling in my stomach as they arrested Peter and John. My thoughts were scrambled with considerations of how I had switched sides in this conflict between the leaders and the followers of Jesus, and also with grave concern about my family and what would happen to us now, without Peter and John.

The sinking feeling quickly rose through my body and stopped in my throat as I felt a heavy hand laid upon my back. I turned and there was my father glaring at me through a mask of anger. "Father," I gasped with no relief from the dread I felt.

"Malchus," he spoke solemnly and with obvious pain, "Caiaphas is going to deal with you—time has run out for you."

"Father, I'm sorry I haven't been to see you, but we have been so caught up in this movement—O Father, Jesus is the Messiah."

Father cut me off abruptly. "No Malchus, he is not, and you are not my son. You are dead. I die to you. I separate from you and your evil. Now I have warned you and I owe you nothing. You are dead." He turned and walked away.

I was stunned, and for a few seconds immobile. Then I saw Caiaphas hurrying into the chambers where the leaders would be meeting to discuss Peter and John. I knew I had little, if any, time and prayed that this confusion would allow me to get a few things out of the house.

It seemed that all the Temple guards were still at the Temple because of the arrest. I sent Bethany and the children to Joanna's house with strict instructions to stay inside. I ran home. Bursting through the door I was relieved that no one had been there yet.

Quickly I went to the room where a stone was loose in the floor and dug up our bag of money. I was going to gather up a few other things, especially some of the family gifts that Bethany treasured, but sensed I should not. I left the house and walked toward the Joppa road away from the Temple. When I had covered about a hundred meters and turned to pass the corner of the city wall, I saw a group of the guards heading toward the house.

I berated myself for being so stupid and not getting the money and some of the treasures out of the house several weeks ago. Soon I came to my senses and thanked God that we were safe—so far—and that at least I had enough money to take care of our needs. I also prayed for Peter and John, and thought that their imprisonment was too high a price to pay for recovering the money.

Bethany and Joanna met me at the door with a barrage of questions. I explained what happened and said, "I was starting to gather some of the family gifts we received at the wedding. I especially wanted to get your grandmother's silver plate, but I sensed I should get out of there fast. I left immediately and went around the city to the west. As I reached the corner I saw a group of Temple guards heading for the house. I'm sorry, Bethany, but all our possessions are gone."

Bethany nodded her head trying to look brave, but the tears were real. She was cut off from the things that give continuity and stability to women. I slipped my arms around her. "I'm sorry, Bethany, that I didn't plan ahead and get our important things out of the house and into a safe place."

She shook her head and held me tightly. "Don't Malchus. Don't blame yourself." We stood still in an embrace for a long time.

Joanna was being careful not to intrude into our time of consolation and encouragement. Noticing her tip-toeing around us, I said, "O Joanna, I'm sorry we just barged in here without any advance notice or asking. I didn't know what else to do and you were the first person that came to mind."

"I'm truly pleased, Malchus, that you sent Bethany and the children here. This is God's house and you are in need. You're welcome to stay as long as you like or as long as is necessary." she replied.

I answered, "Thank you so much, Joanna, you are very kind. I suspect, however, that it can't be for long or we will jeopardize you and your house too."

The children took a long time to calm down. They could sense the trauma, but didn't understand about not being able to go home—ever. Joanna's house was nice, and somewhat large, but we were used to a big house, with panelled walls in the main room. Here we slept on the floor. At home they knew where the water jar was and could help themselves, even in the night. It was difficult for them.

They had been lying on their make shift mats for some time when Sarah came to Bethany and whispered in her ear. Bethany held her for a long time. She took her to the vessel where she could relieve herself, and then laid down with her on the mat.

"It must be tough on them," said Joanna. "Losing their home and the security of relatives and neighbors." Then she looked at me and said, "It must be hard on you and Bethany too."

I knew we had to get out of Jerusalem somehow, and began thinking about possible ways to do it. How difficult it would be depended on how badly Caiaphas wanted to arrest me and make a spectacle of me. I suspected that since he had now made the decision to strike, I would be the place for him to vent his frustration against Jesus and against all the set backs he had suffered as the High Priest.

Bethany fell asleep with Sarah. I asked Joanna, "Is there any place near here where I could get a small piece of parchment to write a note to my mother? I know she will be suffering terribly, and I want to assure her as best I can that we will be all right."

"I have a pen and a few pieces of parchment left from my father. He was an Amanuenses and I have kept it for years. I was planning to give it to the apostles for their use, but you're welcome to use it Malchus."

I was touched at the providence of God that such a rare item would be at hand here in this house. I said, "Let me buy them from you Joanna?"

She responded, "I am going to forget you said that, Malchus, otherwise I would be angry."

There was nothing I could say that would not make it worse, so I kept silent and smiled at her. She brought me the bag with her father's pen, and some scraps of parchment, excused herself and went off to bed.

"Mother we love you greatly and know you must stand with Father. We promise to take good care of your grandchildren. May God reunite us, and reveal Jesus to you and Father as the Messiah. No matter what, we love you.

Malchus and Bethany."

How to get this to Mother? How to get my family to safety? How to not jeopardize my new brothers and sisters for helping us? What will happen to Peter and John?

With my mind filled with these questions, and the constant prayers they evoked, I got down on the floor between Bethany and Jehoiada and fell into a fitful sleep. I dreamed of my childhood in the Temple with the lamb, the priests and the blood, but instead of waking up, I ran from the Temple and was suddenly running up the Mount of Olives again, leading the mob from the Temple. I awoke with a gasp as my ear was cut off.

"It's all right Malchus. It's all right." Bethany was holding me and saying. "We're here at Joanna's house. We're together. It's all right."

She was saying this for her sake, as well as mine. It was all right, but for how long?

CHAPTER FOURTEEN

JERUSALEM

With the rising of the sun came a rising of hope and peace. Our situation was desperate: Caiaphas wanted to arrest me and possibly imprison or sell my wife and children; Temple guards had gone to our house; Peter and John were arrested yesterday; we were "guests" in the house of Joanna, a widow who spent most of her time helping others. There was no reason for this peace and hope, yet it was real. Even the children felt it, and after we had eaten and Joanna left for the Temple, we spent the day playing and talking and trying to keep the noise down so that neighbors would not realize we were there. The hardest task that day was to stay quiet.

The shadows were creeping across the room by the time Joanna returned that afternoon. She started asking us about our situation, but interrupted herself with, "Oh, of course you're all right. Let me tell you what has happened." She bounced from one foot to the other, and kept walking while she talked. "Peter and John had to spend the night in prison. But this morning, when the leaders met to consider their punishment, there were so many people in the Temple, and such an excitement about the man who was healed, and so many of his relatives and friends were there too, they just couldn't do anything to Peter and John except warn them and let them go. And Peter, Peter, do you know what he said?"

I said, "No, Joanna, of course we don't know what he said. What did he say? What did he say?" I was getting as excited as she was.

"He told the Sanhedrin that they killed Jesus, but God raised him from the dead, and it was in his name that the man was healed."

"Whew," I broke in, "They must have been furious."

"Oh, they were, they were. And then they put Peter and John out and talked among themselves. When they brought them back they threatened them and commanded them to stop speaking or teaching in the name of Jesus."

"Peter told them to judge for themselves if it was right to listen to the council, or to listen to God. Then he told them he was going to keep on saying the things he had seen and heard."

"They must have been wild with rage," I said. "Did they sentence them? or beat them? or what?"

"No. There was such a crowd and so much going on at the Temple, they just warned them again and let them go," Joanna continued. "Then, as many of us as would fit, went to that upper room place and prayed. Oh, it was tremendous. They prayed for courage to keep on preaching Jesus, and you know what?"

"Tell us, Joanna, tell us!"

"Well, when they finished asking for courage to keep on preaching, we were all saying, 'Indeed. Grant us all courage,' and things like that and suddenly the whole place shook. We thought it was an earthquake, but nothing else shook around the area. See what happened? God shook the place, God shook the place," she finally finished, or so we thought.

She picked up again, "Oh, and then Peter asked, 'Where's Malchus? Has anyone seen Malchus?' I went to him and told him what had happened, and that you were here. He said, 'Good. Tell Malchus to stay put and not move. I will be there when I can, but under no circumstances should he leave the house.'"

I laughed, "Well Joanna, if I have to be in prison, this is certainly a nice one, and it's good to have my wife and children with me."

The sun was barely brightening the eastern sky when a soft knocking caused us all to scurry around and quickly make the change from sound sleep to wide awake. Joanna cautiously opened the door and there stood Peter with his wife. "Shalom

Eliechim," Peter greeted us. "May the peace of God guide our steps this day."

It was a shock to me to see his wife, I didn't even know he was married. Peter quickly introduced Hannah to us, and I introduced Bethany, Jehoiada and Sarah to Peter and his wife. "My wife has just come up from Capernaum in Galilee," Peter said. "It appears we will be centering our activities in Jerusalem, and I praise God that she can be with me. Now, Malchus, we must talk."

Bethany and Joanna began preparing some food. Peter's wife talked with Jehoiada and Sarah and told them how she missed her children who were still with their grandparents in Capernaum, but should be here soon when she and Peter found a house or made other arrangements. She seemed to enjoy the children and felt secure with them. I suspected that this wife of a former fisherman was having some difficulties with the adjustment of being the wife of the apostle Peter. "Lord help her," I silently prayed, "and keep her from pretending to be something she is not."

Peter wasted no time, "Malchus, John and I overheard several conversations about you, while we were in prison, and during the time they put us out of the room while the leaders met. Guards were asking questions about you, wanted to know what your wife and children look like, and what to do with the things taken from your house. It appears serious brother . . . Caiaphas is a volcano erupting on everyone around him. I think he will try to vent all his feelings on you. You've got to get out of here, Malchus. And soon."

Peter continued, "When we prayed . . . let's see now, it was two days ago, anyway, when we prayed about you, there was a strong sensing of danger and the need to get you out of Jerusalem. That has certainly been proven true. Caiaphas is even now searching for you in various places. Should you show up at the Temple, you would be arrested immediately. I think he will even begin searching, or at least posting a watch on some of the homes of the brothers, in the next few days. Should they find you here, it would be great trouble for Joanna.

"So," he went on, "where should you go? How can you get there? What will you need? And how soon can you go? These are big problems, but let's take care of them."

I began with the money. "We have nothing as far as clothing or furnishings or anything, Peter, but I did manage to retrieve our savings. There is enough here to start out again in another place, but I've been desiring to give it to you and the other leaders to distribute as you see the needs among us."

Peter asked, "Do you really want to give it to God and let me and the other apostles use it?"

There was a time of silence as I considered the implications of this. I would have nothing. I would be dependent on Peter and the other apostles. Actually, I would be dependent on God, and his ability to work through others. "Yes," I answered. "I give this to you," and handed the bag to Peter.

He reached out and took the bag, weighing it up and down in his hand, yet never taking his eyes off me. He finally said, "I receive this, Malchus, in the name of Jesus. It belongs to God and God's people." Then he reached out and handed it back to me. "Take this, Malchus, and use it wisely. Remember, it is God's, not yours—you just have the use of it. Get settled and meet the needs of your family, and then, if there is an excess, share it with those in need at that place. Do you understand?"

Tears filled my eyes as I nodded and hugged this rugged fisherman who so clearly reflected Jesus. Bethany knocked on the door, "Malchus, Peter, come on. The food is ready."

Peter broke the bread, blessed it, and added, "Lord Jesus, we invite you to come and break bread with us. We acknowledge your presence here—you said you would be with us till the end of the age. Lord, give us your wisdom and let us have your mind as we consider the problems facing Malchus and his family. Thank you for the problems Lord, and the chance to bring you glory in overcoming."

"What's going to happen to us, Abba?" Jehoiada asked. "Where are we going to go?"

"We don't know yet son, but we must leave here very soon, maybe even today."

"Or tomorrow," Peter interrupted.

Bethany excitedly broke into the conversation with, "Oh, Malchus, can we go to Joppa?"

"Joppa? What's with Joppa?" Peter asked.

"Seven or eight years ago we went to Joppa on a trip for Caiaphas, and while we were there, we bought some property," I responded.

"Surely Caiaphas knows about it," Peter said. "You have to go someplace where no one knows, or no one can trace you back to Caiaphas."

"Actually he doesn't know about it. No one does," I said, "except a woman there named Dorcas. It was one of those things you do right at the moment, and then wonder about it for a long time. It was so impractical. It's a beautiful piece of property overlooking the sea. We were thinking about a place where Bethany and I could occasionally get away from everything, but it is situated on cliffs and would be dangerous for little children, and there is a constant breeze—Oh, it's perfect," I interrupted myself.

"Perfect? Perfect for what?" Peter asked.

"Tanning hides." I replied. "I was apprenticed as a sandal maker, and I have had some experience with tanning. We could set up a tannery there, where the breeze could keep the odor at a distance from the house, and also isolate us from curious people."

"That sounds great," Peter said. "But is there anything in your house that would reveal you own the property. They will search your belongings very carefully, and also be questioning your families. You must not contact your families, even your father Bethany, what was his name?"

"Asaph," she replied.

"Yes, even him. You should wait for a suitable period of time, and even then not give your location. That will protect him too," Peter said. "Oh, and by the way, what will your name be?"

I had been thinking about this problem for some time and immediately said, "Simon—after you, Peter. Jesus gave you the name Peter, so I would like to take your original name of Simon."

"Simon," he said slowly. "Simon the tanner—it has a nice sound to it. What do you think Bethany?"

"He will always be Malchus to me, Peter, but to others it is a blessed name. I approve," said Bethany.

"So be it, Simon the tanner. Now, no one must know the name or the place you are going except Joanna, my wife and me. Even your friends here, or the ones who help get you out of Jerusalem. Soon Caiaphas will be offering a reward for you, and the fewer that know, the better," Peter said with a great deal of authority. "Now let's make some plans about getting you out of here.

* * *

Bethany and the children left shortly after noon that day. I gave her about half the money with instructions that if I did not meet them at the khan in Beth-horon, she was to proceed to Joppa and stay with Dorcas. Peter had arranged for a couple to come to Joanna's and accompany Bethany and the children.

Bethany, wearing rags and covering her eyes and face, was led by a rope. The young couple from the community of believers led her, and kept the children with them. They cried "unclean," when anyone came near Bethany, and had no trouble leaving the city. Just outside the city, all travelers were being checked by the Temple guards who looked at this couple with the children, then back at Bethany and stepped as far out of the way as possible.

The couple led Bethany for seven or eight hundred rods before they were certain no one was suspicious. Finding an isolated spot, they buried the rags she had been wearing, and quickly proceeded on to Beth-horon and the khan. Tired and worn, they arrived about dusk to begin their vigil of waiting and praying. The couple was prepared to stay three or four days if necessary.

My escape was more intricate.

Joanna and Peter's wife cut off most of my very well trimmed beard. They rubbed chalk in the scraggly remnants and also throughout my hair. Then they took some dark olive oil, mixed it with various pigments and transformed my face about three shades darker. Joanna handed me her mirror and asked, "Well, what do you think, Malchus, I mean, Simon?"

It was a strange feeling to look into a mirror and see someone that looked so very different. I doubt that anyone would have recognized me from my appearance. "You did a good job. No one will recognize me. Thank you. Thank you so very much for everything you have done."

"Please don't get all caught up with thank yous, Malchus," Joanna chided. "It's actually been a lot of fun and a real adventure. Hasn't it Hannah?" she asked Peter's wife.

"Yes," she responded.

They were serious, and I gratefully dropped the matter of thanking them. Now all we had to do was wait until the third or fourth watch in the night.

One of the brothers had been sent to buy an old cart and some very smelly skins from a tanner south of the city. Tanners were not supposed to bring the skins inside the city until the hides were well cured and no longer offensive. He got some very "ripe" skins, and was prepared to bribe the guards for the privilege of passing through the city in the middle of the night rather than going clear around. He had no trouble at all entering the city. Now the problem was for me to leave it.

I had fallen asleep while waiting for the cart, but while still several rods away, the strong smell instantly woke me up. Quickly saying good-bye to Joanna, Hannah and Peter, who had returned to the house, I relieved my suffering brother from his position next to the foul smelling skins. All I had with me was a skin of wine to help with our deception.

I splashed some wine over me, in case anyone got close enough, or could smell anything besides the foul odor of the fresh skins being processed with fresh dung. I had to hurry and get moving along. The odor was so offensive, people would shout at me if it got them out of bed.

I made it through the streets to the gate that led to Beth-horon. No one came out of his house, although I heard several people muttering. As I went through the Joppa gate, I noticed several Temple guards ahead sitting by a fire just off the road.

I headed right for them as if I was going to join them, and began slurring like a drunken man, "O good, a fire, a fire."

The guards were up in an instant and shouting, "Get away you old fool. You shouldn't be here. Move on." They picked up small stones and threw them at me and the donkey to hurry us along.

I kept up the drunken speech and shouted back, "You don't have to be so nasty!" I silently laughed to myself and thanked God for a safe escape. Like Bethany had done with the rags, I also buried the foulest smelling skins a couple hundred rods outside Jerusalem. It was still before dawn, and there were no travelers on the roads. I sang as I drove toward Beth-horon and my waiting family, and the adventures that would surely face us in our new life in Joppa.

CHAPTER FIFTEEN

ROME

$\mathbf{T}$oday is to be my last day here in prison. It's like every other day, but it's different since it's the last one, and also different in that my hand hurts. The skin is pink and puffy around the wound, and the entire hand has swollen. I can not close the fingers because of the swelling, and eating the mid-morning bowl of food is difficult.

As usual, whatever was available was boiled in a pot, slopped in a bowl and slid into our cells at the bottom of the door. Always hungry, we are quick to get the bowl of food and eat it right away so as not to attract the rats which are always willing to eat the stuff. Bold and hungry, they constantly test us to see how close they can come, and how much food they can steal away.

A while ago, as the days just dragged on, I had named several of the rats and even talked to them. Now I am without the luxury of time to spend on such things as my mind is relentlessly reviewing my life, and also I am angry that these same rats fight and test me for this bowl of better than usual food.

My hunger drives me to get some of this gruel into my stomach quickly. My left hand is so clumsy that the first full spoon finds the floor and not my mouth—almost an entire spoonful. "You filthy wretched slimy thing," I snarl at the thieving rat, kicking at him as he scurries off with some of my food. Immediately, other rats head for my bowl. I scoop up the remnants from the floor, dump them back into the bowl and pick it up with my left hand. Steadying it with the heel of my right thumb, I put my face in the bowl of food and munch away like a dog.

It feels so good when the empty aching in my belly is relieved, but now I feel badly because of my barbarous behavior. I begin shivering, "Oh God, I don't understand why you made these vile creatures," I cry out in frustration.

Like a small boat tossed in heavy seas, my thoughts bob back and forth—first one way, then the other. I start to apologize to the Lord, but then wonder what for? I don't know why he made them, and I don't like them. I hate them, especially in the night when they scurry around and even run over my body. Leaving that thought alone, I finish the meager ration, lie back down, and say to the rats, "Go ahead. Eat up. You won't be getting much more from me."

* * *

The rest of the day goes by with me lying down and enjoying each morsel of memory from the Joppa years. They were good years, and the memories are good.

TO JOPPA

Circling wide around Beth-horon, I entered the city from the northwest arriving about midday. I still smelled bad, but it was bearable, and I was not stopped or told to move on, even in front of the khan. The children started to run to greet me, but quickly stopped and looked intently at my altered features. I laughed and said, "Pretty soon I'll look the way I did, but remember now, we have to pretend that I'm somebody else."

As Bethany and the young couple came out to greet me, the curious manager of the khan also approached to find out any news he could. The people at the khans were the best source of information regarding travelers and happenings around the country. Many rewarded them for passing on messages to interested parties, and sometimes the officials would threaten them in order to get wanted information.

I tried to be as offensive and repulsive as possible. "What kind of a place is this?" I demanded of everybody. "I was robbed last night somewhere between Antipatris and Lydda. Has this whole area nothing but a bunch of thieves and robbers? Huh?"

"You're a long way from Antipatris, brother to my husband," Bethany said to me. "And we are not all thieves here, no matter what you might think."

"What are they doing here?" I demanded looking at the young couple.

"The children and I have been visiting my brother in Jerusalem for a week," Bethany said. "They were kind enough to bring us here to meet you and to come with us to Emmaus to help."

I looked at the innkeeper and snarled, "It's not help she wants, she just doesn't want to be alone with me. She's made my brother's life miserable, and now she wants to make me miserable too."

"Tipaulus, I don't want anything to do with your life, and I am not in any way obligated to you," Bethany defiantly said to me. Then turning to the innkeeper she continued, "I am sorry you have been brought into this unfortunate scene, sir. My husband is a cruel and abusive man who is now suffering from leprosy. He has refused to leave the house, and a rabbi in Emmaus suggested we ask his brother to help before we turn him over to the authorities who will have to deal with him forcibly." As she talked, Bethany drew the children close to her for her sake as well as theirs. I was relieved that she did this because the situation had become very tense, and the children needed the reassurance.

"Leprosy!" I shouted. "What do they know? What did they know when they lied and said my father and mother had it?" I could see the fear cloud over the face of the innkeeper.

Then turning to the young couple I snapped, "You can go back to Jerusalem now. I'll take her to Emmaus and take care of everything."

"No, Tipaulus, we had planned to help her through this, and we are prepared to go with you to Emmaus. We will go with you."

I raised my voice feigning anger, "I said you don't have to go and you don't. Now go back to Jerusalem."

Bethany went over to her supposed brother, put her arm in his and said, "I want them to come, Tipaulus. They are a great comfort to me."

Turning to the innkeeper I tried to drag him in, thinking it would drive him off. "Can't you help me make sense to these people. They don't need to come. They should go back to Jerusalem where they came from."

The innkeeper said, "This is obviously a family matter, and I don't see how I could help out."

"Any fool can see," I said raising my voice even louder, "that they don't have to go to Emmaus. They should go back to Jerusalem! Don't you think so?"

By now he was retreating back towards the khan. "Wait," I commanded. "I need to buy some things that were stolen. Clothing. Bedding." Then turning to Bethany I said in a demanding way, "Do you have money for these things? I will pay you back sometime."

The man from the khan said, "No. That's all right. I have some bedding and an old garment I will give you." He quickly gathered some old bedding that should have been thrown out and a garment that was shredded in places.

I took them with a scowl on my face and said sarcastically, "Thank you very much."

He was beginning to get angry and said, "You'd better be getting on your way."

I threw the stuff on the cart, put the very confused and silent children on top of it and sneered at the others, "All right, let's go." I led the way toward the south and west where Emmaus was only about an hour's walk away.

Jehoiada was trying to be very manly for his nine years and remained silent. Sarah, however, at only five was unable to keep it in. She cried as we left, which helped our pretense, but as soon as we were out of hearing I tried to comfort her with words. "We were only pretending Sarah, so that man would not know who we are or where we're going. It will be fine, Sarah. You'll see."

She cried, "Why do we have to pretend Abba? I want to go home. I want to see Grandmama."

Bethany hurried to the cart, got on and held Sarah tightly. "We're going to our new home, Sarah. You'll like our new home, but for a few days we are going to have to make the best of it. Please try to understand."

We arrived in Emmaus in good time and stayed together so if anyone inquired about us, we would not be easily identified as Malchus and family. We went to the market and bought as much supplies and household items as possible without calling undue attention to ourselves. The young couple from Jerusalem stayed with us for a short while, then left for Jerusalem, hoping to get there before nightfall.

We continued shopping and as people began returning to their homes for the evening meal, we headed straight west as if we were also going to a home. When we were well out of Emmaus, heading in a direction that would intersect the road from Mareshah to Lydda, we stopped by some trees and made camp.

The children seemed more secure after a hearty meal and with only the four of us together again. They were getting used to my different looks, and my skin was beginning to show its natural color. They told me all about their trip out of Jerusalem and how they tricked the guards. The more they talked, the more they relaxed.

I related my escape and made a full blown scene for them of pretending to be drunk and how the guards threw rocks at me to get me out of there. We all laughed and had a marvelous time. It was a very pleasant night. I tethered the donkey, turned the cart on its side as a windbreak and we all rolled up in the bedding from the khan and the lamb skins we had purchased in Emmaus. I was grateful for the nice weather. A rainstorm would have made this a miserable night.

We were awakened a little after dawn by a farmer who lived close by. He asked us to go to his home and break bread with him, but I lied and said we had to get to Mareshah as soon as possible. Bethany seemed to have some struggles with our pretenses, but I felt I was doing nothing wrong.

We thanked him, ate some of our food and headed off straight west to intersect the road between Mareshah to the south and Lydda to the north. But our overly helpful farmer ran after us and pointed us toward the south saying that it was easier to get to the road that way, and since we were headed for Mareshah it was on our way anyway. We followed his directions and came to the road in about an hour.

We turned back north toward Lydda and followed the road for a couple hundred rods. When we got close to the place where we would have intersected the road if the farmer had not routed us south, we turned off the main road and headed west again.

The traveling was more difficult this way with many wadis to cross, but our chances of being identified were much less. We headed in the general direction of Ekron, which was on the border of Livia. We tried to make good time without wearing out the children and intersected another main road just north of Ekron about midafternoon. We crossed the road, found a suitable place for Bethany and the children to wait and rest while I went into town to buy provisions.

When I returned with bread, cheese, curds and some pressed cakes, the children had fallen asleep and Bethany was resting against the cart. What a beautiful family, I thought, and what great attitudes they are showing in this difficult journey.

After the rest and the meal, we again headed west and north. When we met the road from Jamnia, we headed north. This road would intersect the main road to Joppa in about three hours, but we had decided to get to the property and not go through Joppa. After almost two hours we left the main road and again headed straight west towards the sea. The area was less settled and harder to travel, so we only went a few hundred rods and stopped for the night.

This night was damp and much colder. The closeness to the sea made a great deal of difference, and although we would get used to it in the years to come, it was a difficult adjustment, especially when sleeping out in the open.

In the morning, we ate and headed directly west, towards the sea. We were travel weary, but high expectations kept us going as we thought the top of each hill would grant us the view of the ocean. For several hours each hill only revealed another hill, or a ravine that we had to circumvent on our quest for the sea and our new homesite.

Finally, when we had begun to think there was no sea, or if there was, we would probably never see it, as we climbed one more hill, a breathtaking panorama unfolded before us— majestic blue ocean, rugged cliffs and crashing, churning, white frothed shore. We stood on the top of that hill with the breeze in our faces for a long time.

Arriving at our own land of promise, shortly afterward, we began walking over our territory like our forefathers had done centuries ago. We blessed the Lord and warned the children. Then warned the children and blessed the Lord.

I gathered my little family around me. "Thank you Lord," I prayed, "for the safe journey to this place of hope. May this land be a sanctuary to us and to many of your people. May it be filled with laughter and praise, and may your holy angels guard us and all the children here from the cliffs and other dangers."

CHAPTER SIXTEEN

JOPPA

The raw beauty of our property and surroundings on the finger of land jutting into the Great Sea was awesome and serene. We quickly forgot the weariness of our travels and the loneliness of separation from family and friends. The small band of travelers had reached its destination—strangers in a strange but beautiful land—unaware of the years of blessing and joy awaiting them.

For the rest of the afternoon we explored every inch of the ground, coast and cliffs. We found enough wood on the beach and the rocks to make a nice fire, and some timbers from shipwrecks we thought would be helpful in building our house. The timbers were too heavy to drag up the cliff, in spite of the relatively easy access from the southwest edge of our land.

Our property was an irregular shape about two hundred cubits north to south with a spit about a hundred cubits wide that protruded into the sea. There were no other nearby neighbors, as the land was rocky and the breezes uncomfortable.

Jehoiada and I gathered rocks and made a small wall on the top of the depression towards the sea. This served as a wind break and made a nice place for our fire and camping. We decided that this would be the spot to build our home with a connected shop just below and to the east. The tannery would be in the hollow further east and south of the house, where we hoped the breezes would keep the odor away from the house. This later proved to be a wise layout of the buildings.

We went to sleep soon after dark on the very spot we chose to build the house. It was wonderful. It was not wonderful just

119

before sunrise when the wind lessened, and the moisture began to settle on everything, including us and our few meager possessions. The depression where we had camped was not only a shield from the wind, it was a small bowl where water collected and quickly formed a shallow pool.

My hand was out from the covers and I awoke with a start thinking it must have rained. My hand was in water—cold water. I pulled it in under the covers again and began the foolish process of self-condemnation for not preparing a booth, or some kind of shelter from the rain. When my senses finally got oriented, I realized it had not rained. My back was wet, and cold, and getting wetter all the time.

I jumped up with a groan and woke Bethany. "Malchus, what's . . . oh no," she groaned as she too sloshed herself out of the water. It was pitch dark. Clouds hid the stars, and there was no hint of light to the east. We knew which direction was east, because of the roaring of the sea in every other direction. We carefully reached out for the children and were relieved to find them still dry.

I wanted to put them on the cart, but Bethany wisely pointed out that as dark as it was, if they turned or fell we would have a terrible time. We felt around enough to become aware of the slope and deposited them where we thought they might stay dry from the water beneath, if not from the water above. Jehoiada began to stir, but quickly returned to his deep sleep.

Bethany and I sat together close to the children where we could help them if they woke. We were wet and chilled and very uncomfortable. We tried to get dry covering over us and keep the wet parts off our skin, but our only real source of heat was one another. Gradually the trembling from the cold stopped. The warmth of our bodies began to melt away the discomfort, the surroundings, the concern about the children, the blackness of the pre-dawn night, the concerns of the past days and the incredible tasks that faced us—all these faded into oblivion as we became one flesh according to the way God designed us.

We lay together as one flesh long after the ecstasy of our passion and need had been fulfilled. The sky in the east began to brighten with an extravagance of color and beauty. "This is

all a sign of the goodness and favor of God upon us, Bethany,"
I said.

"He is so good," Bethany responded. " However long we
have one another, and this place of such beauty, my Lord Mal
. . . , my Lord Simon, I will bless his name and serve him, and
you his servant, with all my heart."

The reality of the situation rudely jolted us as Jehoiada
whined, "I'm all wet. I'm soaked. Uwh, this is terrible." We
scrambled as best we could to get untangled and keep covered,
and also to assure him that it would be all right. "It's only dew
Jehoiada. There's a pool of it just below us. Your mother and
I got soaked, but we moved you and Sarah up out of the water,"
I explained as I rolled and tried to get back into my wet garment.
I let out a gasp from the cold and wet, and Bethany began to
laugh.

Jehoiada continued his whining with, "It's not funny. I'm
all wet."

"I know son," Bethany responded, now a little more sympathetic. "Your father's gasp from the cold and wet made me
laugh. It's really not funny to wake up all wet and cold like
this."

This was all the motherly tenderness Jehoiada needed to
get out of his preoccupation with his own needs and begin to
think of others and of the situation. As he leaned over and made
sure his sleeping sister was covered as much as possible, a
feeling of joy and satisfaction welled up within me. He is
maturing I thought, and becoming manly.

It was impossible to start a fire. The remains of our previous
fire were covered with water. The only thing that seemed to
want to burn was the ends of my fingers where the flint sparks
kept hitting the same place. Everything else was just too wet.
There was nothing to do but wait and hope the sun would dry
things out. Clouds hung in the sky overhead and to the west,
but to the east there was enough clear sky to give us an hour or
two of sunshine.

Once we were all up and had eaten our ration of damp, wet,
cold food, Bethany and Sarah were sent off to Joppa to see
Dorcas and explain our situation. They were also to buy any
supplies and foodstuffs we could keep in our watery condition.

Jehoiada and I set about digging drainage channels, and gathering what we could to get some kind of protection over our heads. The rain would not hold off indefinitely.

Using rocks and pieces of wood, Jehoiada and I were able to cut a drainage channel which left only a small pool of water, but the ground was so rocky it was impossible for us to do any better without proper tools. We concluded that it would be possible to dig, or chip out of the rock, a cistern for our water supply that would actually be inside the house.

Since there were very few trees along the coast, the foraging for branches and poles to fashion a kind of booth was not fruitful. We did better by scouring the beaches to the south. Several trips with torn sail, rigging, and wood scraps had caused a sizable mound of materials to emerge.

About noon, as we were bringing up another load, what seemed to be a small caravan approached our little outpost. Bethany and Dorcas, arm in arm, were in the lead. Sarah was riding on the cart, now piled high with stuff, followed by a man leading another donkey loaded with what appeared to be tents, and bringing up the rear was another donkey and cart with tools, building supplies, two men and a boy.

With their free arms waving, Bethany and Dorcas hurried towards us. Jehoiada and I broke into a run to greet them. "Simon, Simon, how good to see you again," Dorcas said, hugging me as if I were her son. "And you, Jehoiada, come and greet old Dorcas," and before he could protest he was swooped off his feet by this incredible woman in an embrace that included a kiss.

I thought Jehoiada might protest, but he was obviously happy with the greeting. A flood of relief swept through me as I realized God was, in his own special way, providing family to make up for what we had left behind. Dorcas was not my mother, but no one else would have known that, and she quickly filled that void with Bethany and the children.

"Mal . . . Simon this is Bortheus," Bethany said. "He is a tent maker with some of his wares. And this is,—is it James?" She asked one of the other men.

"Yes, Simon, I am James and this is my son Theudas, and my friend Joseph. We have all come to welcome you, and to help in any way we can."

"Yes," Dorcas broke in, "and we have all accepted the glorious fact that Jesus is the Messiah, the promised one of Israel." She laughed with joy.

"Hallelujah, hallelujah," I began shouting. Happiness, joy and a sense of well-being engulfed me. Smiling through tears I raised my arms and continued praising God. "Thank you, Lord, for your goodness and care for all your servants. Thank you that you have provided these brothers and sisters to bless us and lift us up, as they already have. Bless them, O Lord, as they have blessed us. Multiply this back upon them. Thank you that you are Immanuel, that you are here also, with us, and in us, and for us."

I suddenly realized that I had just started praising without considering the others, but when I looked at them, they were all joining in the worship and praise.

Our vulnerable exposure to the elements, and the possibility of rain cut short any further greetings. We got right to the business at hand. First, we selected a tent that would serve us as temporary shelter while our house was being built. We pitched it between the site of the house and the tannery, so that it would not be in the way of our construction.

Bethany and Dorcas began putting things in order inside, Sarah playing nearby. James and the others went to the beach to inspect the timbers while Bortheus and I settled on the price of the tent.

It was the strangest bargaining, or haggling over price, I had ever experienced. I had some idea of a fair price since I knew the value of the skins and could estimate how long it takes to make a tent. Bortheus, however, was not so concerned about getting a fair price as he was about helping out this family in crisis. It was a natural conclusion to think that whatever caused this harsh and abrupt change in our lifestyle also affected our supply of money.

He began the bartering with, "Do you think five shekels would be fair?"

My look of shock and surprise seemed to frighten him, as if he had taken advantage of us. "No, no," I answered. "The skins alone are worth twice that plus the time and effort you spent sewing the tent. Twenty-five shekels."

"No good, no good," Bortheus retorted. "I could not think of taking more than ten at the very most."

"Impossible. I must pay at least twenty three," I demanded.

The haggling went on just like a normal bargaining session, only in reverse. We finally arrived at eighteen. I was pretty certain he could have gotten twenty from a wealthy traveler in Joppa, but eighteen included a fair profit for Bortheus.

Once we finally arrived at a price and payment was made, we embraced and chuckled over this unusual manner of commerce. "You know, Simon," Bortheus said, "when you get the tannery in operation, there is a strong market for skins in Joppa. You can sell the skins at a good price to the merchants who ship them all over from here. There are more goods coming into Joppa than going out, and the wise dealers are looking for ways to take advantage of lower cargo rates."

"I will remember that Bortheus," I responded. "But I had hoped to keep the tannery small, and make sandals as my primary source of income. Yet, who knows?"

Bortheus twisted up his face in a way that said, this didn't make sense, but he wouldn't ask questions. He did say, "Well at least I hope I can buy a few good skins from you for the tents. I welcome you here, Simon, and look forward to working with you in whatever way. Please, now, give my regards to the rest of your family as I must be back in Joppa for some important business. Shalom, Simon."

Thanking God for his goodness and provision, I headed for the beach with the other men. They were just coming up the bank, struggling with a large beam. I joined them in the labor and was soon perspiring with them. It felt good to work hard with these brothers.

James, who worked in various construction projects at the harbor, said the beam would bring a good price, and was really not suitable for a house. He went on about how much money I would gain from the sale of the beam. I protested that God had provided ample finances for us, and that it should be shared by

124

all of us. James finally agreed to this, and Joseph was delighted since he was in debt and had no regular work. The beam was so long, we loaded it on both carts with a long protrusion in the front and back. James quickly harnessed the two donkeys one on each side of the beam, giving us a glimpse of the quality of his skill and craftsmanship, which would become so obvious in the next days and weeks.

James' son asked if Jehoiada could go with them, and James heartily encouraged it. "He can spend the night with us, and we will all return in the morning to get to work on the house. What do you think, Simon?"

Noticing Jehoiada's excitement, and feeling a measure of peace within, I agreed, and the strange looking vehicle with two carts under it, led by two men and two boys, pulled by two donkeys, slowly made its way towards Joppa.

While Bethany, Dorcas and Sarah happily chatted and worked in the tent, I made good use of the tools James had left. First I made an oven outside the tent where Bethany could cook and bake bread. Then I fashioned a covering that could be placed over the oven at night to keep off the dampness. I was just finishing the drainage channel Jehoiada and I had started, when the women came out of the tent with the suggestion of going to Joppa and spending the night at Dorcas'. It was getting late and Bethany didn't want Dorcas to go back alone.

I heartily concurred that they should go, but reminded them that I should not be exposing myself to possible identification. I would remain here and they could go on with Dorcas. Bethany had some misgivings about leaving me alone here, but they were small and I insisted they go on without me. Embracing me warmly Dorcas said, "Malchus, I am so grateful that God has given me you and your family. I feel like I have a family again. I hope you understand." I certainly did.

After they left, thinking I had a little time before dark, I continued working. In a few minutes, however, a gentle but steady rain drove me inside the tent. It was amazing! Comfort, order and warmth surrounded me. The bedding was all together like a couch for sitting. A small stand with a lamp and flint was ready in place. Our clothing and food provisions were neatly stored on one side, and there was a chair. How and when and where did they get that, I wondered.

I ate some delicious bread with butter and cheese, drank a little wine and finished it all off with nuts and a raisin cake. A fitting feast for this palace, I thought. Carefully checking the perimeter of the tent for any places the water might be coming in, I was pleased to see that we had done a good job in pitching the tent. I made my way to the couch of bedding and was going to spend some time praying, but no sooner had I begun speaking to the Lord than I fell sound asleep. I vaguely recall waking up once and putting some covers on me, but the sounds of the sea were like a mother's lullaby, and I slept like a baby.

CHAPTER SEVENTEEN

ROME

T hinking about Joppa—the building of our home there, and the tremendous years that followed—seemed to sweep me into a mood of sadness and loneliness. Tears welled up in my eyes and my heart ached for Bethany and the children. I asked the ravenous questions, questions that devoured my peace and solitude: Are they all right? Do they have any idea of what has happened to me? Do they still have the house and tannery? Does the church still meet there?

Once my mind got on the church that met in our house, I remembered the counsel I had given to so many others. "Give your thoughts and imaginings to the Lord. Don't feed on your self-pity. Get out of it by giving thanks in every situation and recount the Lord's hand and blessing in everything."

This was enough to bring me back to reality. I asked the Lord to forgive me for not practicing what I had preached, and for wallowing in my self-pity. He seemed pleased with this prayer, and I began again to recount the blessings of the Joppa years.

JOPPA

The morning broke, clear and sunny, at our homesite south of Joppa. I was alone. It would be the last time for anyone to be alone at that place. I had barely started the tasks at hand when James and his son, with Jehoiada and Joseph returned with the carts and donkeys, now loaded with building materials. They were a happy lot, and I was most pleased that Jehoiada had obviously enjoyed himself.

"Well, we have much to do to get you in a real house," James began, "but first it's pay time. Here, Simon, this is your share of the beam, less the cost of these materials. It brought a handsome price at the shipyards as they were in need of such a beam for a repair job, and the ship owner was pressuring them to hurry up and get the job done."

I protested, but to no avail. My money was the equivalent of about two months' wages for a worker. James and Joseph had each received the same, and Joseph had been able to pay off his debt which, if not paid soon, would have him put in prison. He said he was broke again, but he owed no man anything.

I said, "Well, I now have enough for some wages for you, if you care to work for me." The instant smile exploding all over his face was his clear answer.

We laid out the basic framework for the house. We planned for a large house, big enough for a large main room and two smaller rooms for Jehoiada and Sarah. To the east of the house, down a few steps, yet still connected to the house, was to be the small shop where I would make sandals. Over the shop was the guest room with access to the roof of our house. The roof was to be built strong enough to be an outdoor area for family and guests with a parapet about two cubits high. On the north side we planned to add a fence, later to form a courtyard.

That first day, we leveled rocky ground, hauled rocks, made framing out of poles, and began plastering the rock walls with a clay like substance that James had brought. By sundown we had a one rock wall started on the entire perimeter of the house, and three rocks high on the west, plus a sizable mound of rocks brought to the site.

James, the builder, was pleased with our progress, and he and his son went home to Joppa late that day. Young Joseph stayed with us that night and "for just a short time to help with the building." He remained for five wonderful years.

Bethany, Dorcas and Sarah returned about noon with some delicious food that Dorcas had prepared. My, how that woman could cook, and how she loved to help others! She beamed with satisfaction as we ate her food. And she seemed to get this same satisfaction when the clothes she made for others fit well and were worn with grace and dignity. She and Bethany were constantly talking, laughing and working together. Dorcas was a great gift from God to all of us.

The next day we worked on the house and shop, but concentrated on the shop where Joseph would stay until the guest room was finished. By the end of the day, there was enough of the wall adjoining the house and the south wall that Joseph could cover his temporary quarters with some of the torn sails we had gathered. He was thrilled with the accommodations and said it was the finest room he had ever stayed in.

Perhaps two unfinished walls and torn sails made the finest room he had ever stayed in, but I felt Joseph was exaggerating. I had noticed other statements from Joseph that were way beyond what was real, and I struggled with my role as his "temporary employer" and the head of the house where he lived. Do I confront the issue? Do I ignore it? What does love require?

I finally decided I must confront the issue, and help this young man. If I didn't, I would not be loving Joseph, and he would become the type of person whose words are discounted. That would be a terrible predicament for one of God's spokesmen, who is to share the ways of the Lord. This habit would rob his words of strength and power.

"Joseph," I cautiously said, "I doubt that it is true that this is the finest room you have ever stayed in. I think I understand why you exaggerate like that, but it makes me worry about the way you speak. You are a follower of Jesus and the words you speak are to be clear and pure. If you exaggerate, the words lose their effectiveness, and you can't be what God wants." I put my hand on his shoulder, looked him in the eye and asked, "Do you understand what I mean?"

He just looked at me. I read the expression on his face as being stunned.

"Joseph, I love you and I want you to be all that God has made you to be. While you're here with us, I want to point out to you the words you say that are exaggerated so you can change the way you speak. Is that acceptable to you?"

Joseph agreed, but I felt that he did it because of me, and not because of this problem. Over the coming months I consistently and lovingly tried to point out to Joseph his carelessness with words. It was a painful process for me, continually calling this to his attention, but the fruit of his life made it all worthwhile.

The day before, James had announced that he had to leave for a job that would take a couple of days, and since it would then be the sabbath he would not return until the first day of the week. I was grateful for his help, and also for an extra day without his motivating example to work so hard. My body ached in every place it could ache, and my struggling attempt to follow his lead and keep up with his work was futile.

After the evening meal, we talked far into the night. It began with Bethany sharing about the times she heard Jesus teach. She described the setting and the feelings so completely that I began to feel as if I were there also. Then, when Joseph asked why we had come to Joppa I answered quickly and turned the attention to him. "Because of our desire to follow Jesus and his way. But, what about you, Joseph? How did you get to this place and circumstance?"

"I was born in Joppa, I think," he answered. "But when I was very young we moved to Caesarea so my father could find work. He died, or was killed working for the Romans, and my mother could not support us. She sold me to a tax collector when I was about six or seven. He was a Jew by name, but he loved the Romans since they gave him the chance to get rich. I hated him from the first day in his house. He beat me and treated me like a pet dog he kept for his children. He treated the dog better than me.

"I did all manner of things for him," Joseph continued, "but the reason he bought me, and the job he trained me for, was to spy on the merchants and traders who came through Caesarea, to find out if they were trying to hide anything from him. I became good at it, and a few times, discovered costly items hidden with grain or even sewn in wine skins. When that happened, he would be kind to me for a few days, but there was never any other reward, and even his kindness was short lived. I tried to run away several times, but he always found me. The tax collectors are everywhere and they help each other out. When I was brought back, he beat me so severely I almost died."

"How did you finally get away?" Jehoiada asked.

Joseph paused for a moment, then continued. "Well, one day when I was snooping around a caravan, some hired workers beat me up and left me injured just outside of Caesarea. I was about twelve years old. A woman who lived near-by saw me and had her husband, a priest, come and get me. I stayed with them for two days, then her husband took me back home.

"The priest hated tax collectors and entered into a big argument with my master concerning my being instructed in the law. Since he was a priest and could make trouble for my master, I was allowed to go to the synagogue once in a while. It wasn't often or regularly, but I was sent just enough to stay out of trouble with the local officials.

"I heard about the law that said you had to set your slaves free in the seventh year, and foolishly told my master about it. That finished my training in the synagogue, but I remembered the law well, and began figuring as best I could when the seventh year would be. The next two years were terrible, but I didn't run away because I knew I could get free sometime around Passover when I was fourteen, I think that was my age."

We had followed every word this young man spoke and encouraged him on with the story. He continued, "The week before Passover I was sent out to check caravans as usual, but instead, I went to the elders of the city and told them my story, emphasizing the harsh treatment and the way I had to spy against my fellow countrymen.

"They hated tax collectors anyway, and told me to stay there with them. A few hours later my master came looking for me, and the elders of the city upbraided him for keeping me, an Israelite slave, beyond the seventh year and for not training me in the law. He was furious, so were they, and a big argument took place. It got so bad the Romans came. My master realized he could loose everything if he lost the favor of Rome.

131

"So," Joseph continued, "I was set free. I had no contact with my mother or any other family. I thought we came from Joppa, so to Joppa I went. I wandered the streets and looked for familiar faces. I slept anywhere, ate anything and tried to get work, but no one hired me. I had no trade, and I didn't know how to do anything except sneak around and spy on people.

Joseph was caught up in his own reverie now. "Finally, one of the very merchants I had exposed to my former master, hired me to work in his business. He bought and sold merchandise—any merchandise he could get cheaply and sell for more than he paid for it. He didn't care where it came from, or who bought it, as long as he could make a profit, and preferably a profit that the tax collectors didn't know about.

"I slept in the permanent stall he operated in Joppa near the harbor, and kept it clean and in order. Sometimes I sold merchandise, and a few times I went with him on caravans to buy or sell. I don't think he had ever forgiven me for turning him in to my former master. He loaned me money at different times, but he kept a record of every cent. Slowly I got into debt. He charged interest, and I was never able to get out of debt. I think he was planning to sell me for the debt and make a lot more money. He was not happy when James and I paid him yesterday, and made him give a receipt."

"That's some story, Joseph," I said, though I didn't believe the whole thing. "How did you get to know Dorcas and James?"

"When I got to Joppa, I went to the synagogue where I hoped I might find my mother. I watched everyone, and looked hard at their faces. Some became uncomfortable, and pretty soon the synagogue ruler came to me and asked what I was doing. After he had heard my story, he said he was sorry, but he didn't know about anybody that could have been my mother, or part of my family. He then said he wanted me to meet a certain lady."

We all interrupted him saying, "Dorcas?"

"Yes, Dorcas. She invited me to come and share the Sabbath meal with her the next week, and when I came, she had made a tunic for me. I often went there and found love and warmth I had never known. She is my only real family."

"Now us too," Jehoiada broke in.

132

"That's right Joseph," Bethany said. "Dorcas is family to us also, so that means we are family too."

I suspected fifteen-year-old Joseph had been trying to stay in control of his feelings and appear strong and manly, but when Bethany spoke those words, his strong exterior crumpled and he began to cry. He got up to leave the tent. Bethany stood also and embraced this young man as if he were her own son. Little Sarah followed her mother and grabbed one of Joseph's legs, and said, "I love you, Joseph." I smiled as I realized he was trapped into a family that loved him, and from which there was no escape—of course, he did not want to escape.

The following day we were just getting started on the building when Sarah came running to us, "Abba, Abba, come and see. There's a big animal on the beach. Come Abba, come see."

Jehoiada, Joseph and I hurried down to the shore where Bethany was still watching the dying animal. It was barely out of the water on an outcropping of rocks. Every few minutes it raised its head and, looking towards us, made a hissing sound. "Oh, Malchus, what is it?" Bethany asked.

I was shocked that she called me Malchus and looked quickly at Joseph. He wrinkled his brow and looked to me for some kind of explanation. I said to Joseph, "My name is now Simon, and since you are part of our family, I will explain the other to you later, and why I had to change it." My anger was apparent in my voice.

Then turning to Bethany, I started to speak, but before I could say anything she said, "I'm sorry Simon, it just burst out with my excitement about this animal."

The anger began to drain away with her sorrow and obvious fear for what she had done. "It's all right," I assured her, and myself also. "This is a good warning for us about how easy it is to use that name. It's good it happened here with only our family."

"Anyway," I continued, "I think this is a sea cow, and the skins of these animals may be what our ancestors used for some of the tabernacle in the wilderness. They must have had many of them in Egypt." Then I raised my voice and in a more formal way said, "We will begin the tannery of Simon the tanner with

133

the skins of the sea cows which the Lord our God brings to this place."

Our little family assembled there on the shore cheered at this announcement. Bethany responded, "So be it, Lord."

But then as I picked up a large stone with which to kill the sea cow, Sarah protested, "Abba, are you going to hurt this animal?"

Stopping this harvesting of God's provision for a moment, I said as tenderly as I could, "Sarah, this animal is sick and is going to die. I'm going to kill it and put it out of its misery. God made these animals for us so we could use their skins. I hope many of them come here, and I will kill them and prepare their skins for sale."

Turning away and heading back towards the tent Sarah said, "I don't want to watch, Abba." Bethany went with her.

I did a poor job of killing the sea cow, which bellowed and thrashed about for two or three good blows to the head. I realized I would have to get better at this. Then I showed Jehoiada and Joseph how to skin the animal. It was interesting and new to me. This sea cow had a layer of fat that was different from that of the sheep and goats I had skinned in the past. It was still, however, a bloody job.

We threw the entrails and pieces of the body into the sea, and many fish quickly assembled to feed. We also noticed a few other sea cows in the area which fed on the fish. We talked about the ways of God, about the animals he created, and how they fed on one another. It struck me that this was the best way to teach Jehoiada, and now Joseph, not only a trade, but also the ways of God as we worked together and spoke about these things.

Next, we gathered the dung from the donkey droppings and smeared it on the inside of the skin. We did this at the spot we had picked for the tannery. Both boys were a little hesitant about this part of the job, but when we finished we washed in the ocean which seemed to keep us partially free from the usual stench that clings to tanners.

By the time we had finished, and made some plans for the manure pile, the racks for drying, and the beginnings of the tannery, it was well into the afternoon. Instead of setting to

134

work on the building projects, we volunteered our services to Bethany who was hurriedly getting ready for our first sabbath in Joppa. There were plenty of tasks to do for her, and soon Dorcas came walking to our home with candles and shawls for Bethany and Sarah. She simply announced that she would be spending the sabbath with us.

Confidence and security seemed to grow in our children, and in us also, as we followed the ancient rituals we had followed in Jerusalem at the sabbath dinner. The candles, the blessings, the meal and fellowship were warm yet mystical. We may be separated from family and living in a tent by the crashing and roaring of the sea, but we are the same we have always been. We are the people of God, marked and set apart by the sabbath.

As usually happened at Joppa, the conversation turned to Jesus, his kingdom, and his teachings. We laughed, talked, prayed and sang, then talked, laughed, prayed and sang some more until one by one we fell asleep—first Sarah, whom we carried to her corner of the tent and covered; next Jehoiada who was already lying on his bedding; then Joseph whom we maneuvered over near Jehoiada; finally Dorcas fell asleep and we covered her next to Bethany, who also fell asleep almost immediately. When I looked for my place to sleep, there was no more room, so I made my way to the unfinished shop where I took Joseph's place.

"Thank you, Lord, for your love and presence and this family that you have made, and also have chosen to be a part of. You are so good, and I love you and appreciate it all," my heart overflowed with thanksgiving. Then I added with a laugh, "And thank you for always being awake, and for listening to me. I love you, Lord."

Clearly and distinctly, yet I don't know where in my being or how, I fell asleep hearing the words, "Thank you son. I love you too."

CHAPTER EIGHTEEN

ROME

The aching in my back calls my thoughts back to my imprisoned body. For hours I have been lying on the hard bunk without moving. I moan and get up to stretch. I had forgotten about the wound until I stood up and each beat of my heart registered a throbbing pain in my right hand. "What a mess. I'm falling apart," I think to myself. "I need a good Sabbath's rest to ..."

The incongruity of my thoughts shocks me. Yet I still speak aloud to no one, "This is the Sabbath. One day is just like another here. Huh. At least if I die tomorrow, I get to die on the day Jesus rose. But if I'm to be crucified, I probably won't die tomorrow. It usually takes two or three days to die by crucifixion. If they cover me with pitch and burn me, I'd die right away. If they put me in the arena with wild animals, death would come soon. The animal that eats me will probably get sick because of my hand. Ha." I begin to laugh at the thought of the animal getting sick because it ate me. "I wonder if I'm going crazy? Who cares?"

"Lord," I pray, "let me go back to that first Sabbath at Joppa, and escape this place for awhile."

JOPPA

It was hard, that first Sabbath morning, not to work on the building for the house, or the tannery, or go kill and skin another

136

sea cow that I spotted on the beach, but it was the Sabbath, and we always rested on the Sabbath. Bethany assumed we were going to Joppa for the synagogue service, and told me, "Hurry up, Simon, we won't get to the synagogue on time."

"I'm not going, Bethany," I said. "I don't think it's wise for me to be in places like that where I might be recognized. It's just a days' journey to Jerusalem, and I need to avoid crowds and places where I might be recognized." Anger rose within me, but I did not stop and examine where the anger was coming from.

"We have always gone to the synagogue on the Sabbath," Bethany returned with what I took also to be anger. "It's part of our faith, part of our religion. We have to go the synagogue on the Sabbath."

"No, we don't," I answered with a rising volume in my voice. Now Dorcas, Joseph and the children were listening. "Even if the law of God commanded us to assemble for synagogue worship on the Sabbath—which it does not do—we would still not have to live by that law because Jesus set us free. But the fact is, the Sabbath is the day of rest, not the day of worship. We get to enter into the rest of God. He worked for six days, made man, and we participate with God as his own by resting with him on this day."

I continued, now almost shouting, "We meet together for synagogue meetings only because it's convenient to do it on the Sabbath since we're not working anyway. We could pick any day to meet, and I cannot meet with the crowds at the synagogue in Joppa, and I won't."

"You don't have to shout, and you don't have to get so angry," Bethany shot back. "Sometimes you're so stubborn and hard-headed, I can't stand it."

"Fine," I retorted. "You and whoever wants to go, go. I'm staying here." I finished the argument by walking over to the edge of the cliff and sitting down as if to watch the ocean. I really wanted to sort out my thoughts and find out where this anger was coming from.

Bethany, Dorcas and Sarah went to the synagogue in Joppa; Jehoiada, Joseph and I stayed at home. I don't know what they did, but I just sat there and tried to get my internal life back in order. I realized that my first flush of anger was because Bethany assumed I would do something and did not talk to me about it. I realized I was being petty by not taking her perspective into consideration. She naturally assumed we were going, and I got angry when she told me to hurry up. I felt some relief at the understanding of what happened, and made up my mind to apologize when she returned.

But two more revelations came to me as I sat there. These were more troubling. The first was the cause of my irritation about the Sabbath and the meaning of the Sabbath. We, Jews, had become religious about Sabbath observance, and had become more conscious of the rules and regulations than of the meaning. The other revelation was that over time the emphasis had switched from resting with God, to meeting with others. The synagogue service became the delight of the Sabbath instead of entering into the rest of God as one of his own people.

Many of my strong feelings about Sabbath were there before I became a follower of Jesus, but now that I was one of his disciples, I took what Jesus said as crucial. He said the Sabbath was made for us, we weren't made for the Sabbath. Also the Sabbath laws were the primary issues the Pharisees used to condemn Jesus.

Even though I knew I was right about the Sabbath emphasis on rest and not worship, I was troubled that I became so adamant and harsh in defending my position. I did not have to be angry and my harshness did not help anyone grasp the liberating freedom of the proper understanding.

If I enter God's rest from his labors in creation, and if I enter his rest of salvation through the work of Jesus the Messiah, why do I get so worked up about it? It did not make sense for me to be so agitated and defensive. "Enter the Sabbath rest, Malchus," I told myself, "and stop being so afraid and frantic about convincing others to understand it."

Fear was somehow at the root of my Sabbath tirades, and fear was the other upsetting revelation. Was I afraid of being discovered? Was I afraid of being brought back to Caiaphas and of dying? It was right for me to be concerned about the family, and not to take unnecessary risks, but was I afraid? Did

I want to save my life? Jesus had said that if I tried to save it, I would lose it.

"Lord," I prayed, "help me to fear no one but you, and fear no situation except that which would displease you."

I got up and called the boys to me. They came slowly, still confused about the argument with Bethany. Jehoiada was not accustomed to such confrontations. "Jehoiada, Joseph," I said seriously, "I want you boys to know that what I said about the Sabbath was right, but my attitude was wrong. I spoke in anger and in fear, and I will ask my wife's forgiveness. But I ask you to forgive me for setting such a bad example as a husband and father."

Jehoiada wanted to smooth it over, just as I did when Peter sought my forgiveness. "It's all right, Father."

"No Jehoiada, it's not all right," I responded. "Please forgive me, and please say that you forgive me."

"I forgive you, Father."

I looked at Joseph.

"I forgive you too, Simon. And I thank you for this example. You are the finest man I have ever met," he said as his eyes filled with tears. We reached out at the same time and embraced one another.

I reached out and pulled Jehoiada into our embrace.

When Bethany and Sarah returned, Bethany and I almost started another argument after each of us asked forgiveness of the other. (Then the issue was: whose fault was it? I said it was my fault, she said it was hers. We each tried to take the blame.) Little did it matter whose fault it was after the Lord clarified the issues, and his forgiveness reigned in our lives.

* * *

Early the next morning I killed and skinned the other sea cow. I had just finished washing up when Jehoiada and Joseph joined me to start work and James and his son came along the path towards the house ready to work also.

"Whew," James exclaimed, "it stinks back along the path. It doesn't smell so bad here, but what is that horrible odor?"

"That's the tannery, James. All tanneries smell like that, but this one is perfectly located because it doesn't smell here at the house, and the breeze keeps the odor away." We then explained how we found the sick sea cow and started up the tanning process the day before the Sabbath.

Within a few weeks, we had built the house and shop with the upstairs guest chamber. Joseph was the permanent occupant of the guest room, except when Peter or other brothers came from Jerusalem. Then, Joseph shared Jehoiada's room, or slept in the small stable we had built near the tannery. The tannery was in operation with several sea cow skins being processed. We were averaging about ten sea cows a week, plus one or two donkeys or goats that people from Joppa and the surrounding area sold us.

Word spread quickly that we had a tannery in operation, and since the only other tanner was some distance north of Joppa, most people sought us out when an animal died. The way it usually worked was that they came to the tannery and we set a price. The next day, Joseph, or sometimes Jehoiada, went to pick up the entire carcass, or just the hide if the animal had already been skinned. The boys paid the agreed price if everything was as represented. We always picked up the animals the next day, unless it was a Sabbath.

After building the house and getting the tannery in operation, there was still considerable money left in our treasure stash. I tried to manage it for the Lord, and give as much to the poor and needy as possible. I did it in such a way that it did not harm their personal integrity, and most of those I helped paid the money back later. Every need that was brought to our attention, we met, but the harder I tried to give the money away, the more we prospered in the tannery or with other salvage items that washed up on the shore. Consequently, our stash of money was getting larger instead of smaller. Dorcas was my best resource for finding people in need, but her requests were usually small. I put many men to work either in the tannery or making sandals, but the more I did, the more I prospered.

I was officially known as Simon the tanner, but I didn't do any of the tanning. Joseph and Jehoiada, and some of the other men did the actual work of tanning. I made sandals in the small

140

shop. There was always an apprentice or two, and men who needed counsel, prayer, or help. Sandal making was a sideline that allowed us to nurture the people the Lord brought to us.

Within a few weeks, we met together as a church in our house. At first, it was in the evening during the middle of the week. All the believers also went to the synagogue every Sabbath except for Jehoiada, Joseph, and me. No one thought that odd, since we supposedly smelled like tanners. After a few months, however, a sharp division arose within the synagogue, between the followers of Jesus and the others. The followers of the Way, as we were called, were cast out of the synagogue, and from that time we met house to house, and in larger gatherings as we had opportunity.

About forty believers came regularly to the tannery on the Sabbath, as well as during the week, and another forty or so met with James, at his house. James and I discussed getting a meeting place where we could all meet together, but the Lord was adding to our numbers so quickly it was soon impossible to find any one place that could accommodate the Church at Joppa. We had to trust God regarding the configuration of the Church and the different flocks that made up the Church of Joppa.

The flock which I shepherded gathered about midmorning on the Sabbath. They usually complained of the smell, but once they got into the house it was never mentioned again. It was noisy and wonderful, reminding me of the festival of Tabernacles when our family came together from all over Israel and lived in booths in our yard. There was the same kind of talking and laughing and playing among the children.

Making sure that no one was sitting by himself, I let this time of sharing go on for about an hour before calling the people together. There were usually good-natured complaints like, "Oh, do we have to start already?" But once we started, the same thing happened when we finished a time of worship, or when a teaching ended, or if we spent time praying for each other. These people were so happy with everything that went on, they would have kept going all day—and sometimes we did.

I would gather two or three of the other men, and pray about the meeting. After making sure our hearts were right with God, and with each other, we asked the Lord to reveal his will to us for the meeting. Once we sensed the direction for the day, we called the people together.

We usually sang psalms, hymns and spiritual songs for about an hour. During that time either there were prayers or prophetic messages, or someone shared a scripture or an encouragement. We felt especially blessed when the Lord spoke a specific word of encouragement, correction or direction through one of the brothers. There was a real bonding together as the family of God. And we sensed that God, our Father, also enjoyed the meetings.

I requested everyone who played an instrument to bring it to the meeting. I wanted them to follow along with the leader. Some played cymbals and tambourines, others flutes and lyres. Perhaps we weren't qualified as Temple musicians, but I thought the music was outstanding. Bethany played a flute, Jehoiada was getting proficient on the lyre and Sarah kept rhythm with two small cymbals. She performed well for a five-year-old.

I always had a lesson or some teaching prepared. Usually, however, I did not get to deliver it. Once it was almost five months before I shared it with my flock. People shared what God had done for them, and others picked up on the theme and contributed to the meeting. Also three of the men were obviously called by God to shepherd or lead in the Church, and I encouraged them to participate. I liked it best when everyone present shared in the meeting in some way. All three of the future leaders frequently gave short teachings. My duty was to keep everything focused in the direction God had set for the meeting, and when it followed that course, it was magnificent.

Sometimes a visitor would tell his tale, like Saul of Tarsus did when he was with us. He had been a Pharisee who persecuted followers of the Way. Jesus appeared to him on the road to Damascus and Saul was changed. After spending a few years in the wilderness, he started preaching about Jesus. He caused a lot of trouble, and the believers didn't trust him. Peter and the others sent him back to Tarsus. He booked passage on a ship from Joppa and stayed here for two weeks while waiting to leave.

Saul visited us one Sabbath, and James' group the next. He spoke for hours, and even after he left we spent many weeks chewing and digesting the rich banquet he had spread for us.

James and I met at least once a week to pray and check with each other. We also often went together to pray for the sick. Whenever possible, we had the upcoming leaders with us, to help them prepare for their leadership. Also, since we, ourselves, lacked experience, we appreciated their help.

When a brother or sister in the Lord was sick, they sent for us and we anointed them with oil in the name of the Lord. Peter and some other apostles had come down from Jerusalem and suggested we follow the pattern they used—to anoint with oil in the name of the Lord, listen to any confession of sin from the sick person, and pray for healing. Whenever the sick person was not healed, the whole community would fast and pray, and seek the Lord's will until He either revealed the hindrance, or healed the sick person. Sometimes, the Lord used sickness in individuals as a means of correcting the whole church.

One time a beloved sister called for us for prayer. She was suffering from chills and fever, and could not stop shaking. We ministered to her, but there was no relief. Before we could call the community to fast and pray, we were summoned to the home of another family where an older child had the same symptoms. Again, after ministering to the child and his family, nothing happened. As usual in this kind of situation, I grew angry and depressed and doubted our assignment from the Lord to heal the sick.

Before the day was over, word had spread throughout the Church of Joppa, and believers all over the city humbled themselves before God, with fasting and prayer. Many gathered in small groups in various houses. Soon after dark, James sent a messenger to me to tell us that one of the brothers had seen a vision of a particular warehouse near the dock, where goods were stored. It happened to be the storage facility that Bortheus used for his tents.

Soon after that, a new believer who had come to our house said, "I don't understand this, but I am seeing something as if I were dreaming while awake."

"Don't be concerned or act strange," I said as he looked at me with his eyes opened extra wide and an expression of amazement on his face. "The Holy Spirit is giving you a vision. It's like prophecy, or I think it's a form of prophecy, but anyway, what are you seeing?"

"I see a pile of tents and behind them, uh, underneath one of them, I see a treasure chest . . . now the treasure chest is open . . . a bright light is shining out. What does it mean Simon?"

"I'm not really certain," I answered, "but I think it goes together with the vision that James told us about in his message. I want you to come with me." Turning to the others in the room I said, "The rest of you keep praying."

I took the brother with me to James' house. We told James what had happened and he joined us to go to Bortheus' house. From there the five of us went to the warehouse. Others wanted to come, but we felt it would draw too much unwelcome attention.

A guard had been posted at the door of the warehouse, but after Bortheus identified himself, we were allowed to go in. Taking a lamp with us, we made our way to the area where Bortheus had a large number of tents awaiting shipment to Rome. The new brother got all excited and said, "This is it! This is what I saw! And there, over there, you'll find the treasure."

We went to the place he indicated, removed the tent, and there, shaking with chills and fever, was a young man in rags who appeared to be a runaway slave. He was delirious and unable to talk, so we put him between James and the new brother, our two strongest, and carried him out.

We decided that best place for this "strange treasure" was in the safety of the tannery, and took him there on one of James' carts. The word was passed among our people to pray for this young man, and to thank God for the treasure he might be.

Some had high expectations from this runaway slave, who was revealed to us as a treasure. There were dreams and speculations of wealth—perhaps this was some great prince who had been stolen away, and a reward was offered for his return. Maybe he was destined to be a great apostle or prophet.

It was Dorcas who brought us back to reality. She reminded us that Jesus said that whatever we did for the least we did for him. In her interpretation the young man was probably one of the least important in the world. To us, though, he was a treasure, because, through him, we had the opportunity to show what we would do for Jesus in such a situation.

CHAPTER NINETEEN

ROME

The setting sun was announcing the end of the Sabbath—time to resume work. O, how I yearn to work! For me it means I have finished my last Sabbath on this earth, or at least my last Sabbath as a follower of Jesus. I hear Cleomus come on duty, and he soon makes his way to my cell. "Malchus, are you all right?" he asks. "I heard about your hand."

"I'm all right, thanks, Cleomus."

"I'm sorry it happened, Malchus. I shouldn't have left the bag with you."

Am I hearing right? Is this for real? Did Cleomus, the hardened Roman soldier, killer of Demetrius, angry, contentious, and mean, really say he was sorry? I look at him and see genuine concern and sorrow written on his face. I am so choked up with emotion, that I can't speak. With a closed mouth smile I nod my head in an attempt to communicate, and as I do, tears splash from my eyes. Finally I manage, "Thanks, Cleomus. Thank you for your concern."

Cleomus turns abruptly and leaves.

Now the weeping finds expression as the dam of my resistance is broken. I think my tears are just for the changes in Cleomus, but as I cry, I imagine holding Bethany in my arms. I can feel her warm, soft body next to me, and I cry. I can see Jehoiada, now a man, probably with children of his own that I will never see, and I cry. I picture Sarah, now a woman, probably married to one of the young men from the community in Joppa, and I cry. Maybe they were all arrested and are in the same predicament as I am.

146

My crying continues until I feel some concern about my example to the prisoners. I listen closely to hear what is happening in other cells. Though it is early evening and the time we often talk to one another, there are few sounds, only unmistakable sobbing and crying coming from several places. I sense my brothers are brave and will die rather than reject their faith in the Lord Jesus, but just like me, the feelings of helplessness and foreboding spill out in bitter-sweet tears.

JOPPA

After bringing the sick young man home, we set out a mat for him in our main room so our "treasure" could be near the fire and close to the nursing care of Bethany. It reminded us of old Bartholomew in the main room of our house in Jerusalem. It took two days before the fever broke enough for him to come to his senses, and begin to realize where he was. He looked like an empty sack with bones sticking out. His eyes, feverish, red and blood-shot, peered at us with the intensity of a trapped animal. He did not want help, but was too weak to protest.

Bethany ignored his feeble protests and lovingly nursed him until his fever broke and he began to gain strength. We moved him into the guest room with Joseph who was to share the love of Jesus with him, as soon as possible. He would then disciple this young man in the ways of the Lord, and the ways of the tannery. Our "treasure" was afraid of everyone and everything, and did not respond well to Joseph. There was a language difficulty, and the young man did not seem to want to learn.

At this point, we decided to move him to Bortheus' home where several languages were spoken, and the family expressed a desire to help draw out our "treasure" as he was called. Gradually, he regained strength, but kept his distance from all who tried to help him.

After a few weeks, our treasure disappeared.

Again, it was Dorcas who kept us on an even keel. Some of the brothers were angry that this young man should be so ungrateful in the face of all our efforts and attempts to love him. She said, "Maybe it was an angel of God just testing us. Or maybe all our imaginations about him are true, but we won't know for sure until we get to paradise. Or maybe he was just a worthless, frightened, runaway slave that Jesus wanted us to love. Jesus will count it as done for him, unless we ruin it with our complaining."

* * *

Those years in Joppa were glorious. The Church of Joppa was a mixture of people from every occupation and social level, yet we were one. We were the family of God and a people counted worthy to follow Jesus and even to suffer for his sake. Many lost their work because they followed the Way, some of us lost family, and a few were even beaten as they were put out of the synagogue. Most of us now shared our homes, at least temporarily, with brothers and sisters fleeing the persecution in Jerusalem. Yet, when we were together there was no evidence that we were suffering.

Anytime two or three of us met, it was a church meeting, and the meetings were like parties. We all sensed that Jesus enjoyed these get-togethers and celebrated with us. James pointed out that creation appeared to be a party. When God spoke out of the whirlwind, he challenged Job with, "Where were you when I laid the earth's foundation? While the morning stars sang together and all the angels of God shouted for joy?" James' conclusion was that God and the angels behaved much as we did.

A new follower of the Way, who had been a Pharisee— some thought he still was—said, "You are not serious enough about the things of God. You are much too foolish and silly in your gatherings, and you offend me, James."

Bortheus pointed out that Solomon also described creation like a big party. He said that wisdom was the craftsman at God's side when God marked out the foundations of the earth, and that wisdom was filled with delight in God's presence day after day. Wisdom rejoiced in God's presence over creation and over mankind. Together, God, wisdom and the host of heaven laughed, danced and played.

He added, "Jesus is wisdom, and when Solomon talks about wisdom, he is talking about Jesus. So you see, brother," Bortheus turned to our resident Pharisee, "creation took six whole days because every time God created, they all had a party and celebrated. God started it by saying, 'It's good! It's good!' then they all started cheering and congratulating God for the good job he had done. Each day the party lasted till the next day, and that's why it took six days, and that's why God rested on the Sabbath—he was tired from all the partying."

We all laughed and heartily agreed, but the religious brother was angry and said, "You will all be sorry you don't show more honor for the things of God. Your meetings are disrespectful, and I can no longer tolerate them." Elevating his nose enough to look down at us and locking his neck in that position, he walked away.

We would have been better off if he had stayed away. Unfortunately, he continually returned to judge us and accuse us and uphold the law of Moses. We didn't know how to deal with him, so we tried to love him into the freedom we were experiencing in Jesus. It appeared to be a mistake, but who knows?

About that time Dorcas became ill. This was a blow to the entire community because she was the one who made sure all the needs of the poor and the widows were known to the leaders. Many people suffered without the help we could have given, but with Dorcas sick, we just didn't know their needs. We brought Dorcas to our house where Bethany could look after her.

It seemed that Dorcas was improving, but before dawn, one day, Bethany shook me from a deep sleep. She was almost hysterical. "She's dead, she's dead. O Malchus, Dorcas is dead, and she's not supposed to die yet. I just know it. It isn't right. O Malchus, what can we do? Dorcas is dead. She's dead."

No words would make any difference at that moment, so I just held Bethany while she continued. After several minutes of incongruent thoughts pouring out of her, Bethany was back in control of her thoughts and actions.

No matter if it was Dorcas' time to die or not, she was dead and certain things had to be done. The body needed washing and the community should be informed. We didn't want to leave her remains in the main room, so I roused Joseph from the upstairs guestroom and sent him to Joppa to tell James and the other leaders.

When Bethany had finished washing Dorcas' body, I carried the remains of this saintly woman to the upstairs guestroom and gently placed the body on the mat. She looked as if she were in a sound sleep, but she wasn't. She was definitely dead.

People began arriving soon, and it seemed that everyone had a story about Dorcas helping them. Some even brought articles of clothing she had made. Bethany kept insisting that she was not supposed to die, but most people just ignored her words as the grieving of one who loved Dorcas and sought to give comfort. Most of us tried to comfort others, and all were in need of solace, for Dorcas had a big place in every heart in Joppa, even amongst the non-believers.

When James came, he took a keen interest in what Bethany was saying about Dorcas not supposed to die. He listened intently and then said, "You know there have been some outstanding miracles taking place through the apostles, and Peter himself is just down the road in Lydda. If you're right, Bethany, who knows what might happen. Let's go down to Lydda and ask Peter to come back with us. We could get there and be back by midafternoon. What do you think, Simon?"

I wasn't as convinced that Dorcas shouldn't have died, but I didn't want to make light of Bethany's conviction or James' faith, so I said, "Let's send some of the brothers."

We all prayed together that God would have his way about Peter coming and that the brothers would find him right away. Also we asked the Lord to be here at the tannery and with all the people who were coming to mourn for Dorcas, just like when he came to Lazarus' funeral and wept with those who mourned. James then added, "And Lord, if you want to raise up Dorcas just like you did Lazarus, please do it."

My faith was strengthened and I felt a little ashamed for not responding to Bethany with the kind of faith and expectation that James exhibited. James, Joseph and one other brother were sent on their way. I went to find Bethany in the guestroom and to encourage her and share with her the prayer and the plan for bringing Peter. "Oh, Mal . . . Oh, Simon, I think the Lord is going to raise her back to life," she said as a gleam cut through the tears in her eyes and a smile began to push away the gloom on her face.

The brothers got back just after noon, and there was Peter, walking along the path to our house. I felt a rush of warmth and tingling as my spirit soared at the sight of this unusual apostle/fisherman. "Peter, Peter," I shouted as I ran to embrace him.

"Simon, how good to see you," he boomed. Embracing Bethany he said, "and even better to see you, Bethany. I would ask how you are, but the brothers have told me about you, and I can see from your faces, in spite of the red eyes, and this beautiful house that all is going well. Praise God!"

Before any more conversing could be done, the brothers and sisters swarmed around Peter and drew him to the upstairs room where the body of Dorcas was lying. They showed him the robes she had made, and other pieces of clothing. Many talked at the same time telling of the wonderful things Dorcas had done, but Peter was able to get the message in spite of all the confusion. Finally, he raised his hands over his head and loudly commanded, "Enough, enough! I understand what you are saying. Everybody get out, and pray that God will be glorified." Then to James and me he said, "You two stay here with me and pray."

I am certain I prayed because Peter commanded it, but I watched carefully what was happening. James and I stood near the door, while Peter went over near the mat. He knelt down on the floor and prayed aloud. It was aloud, but it was so quiet I had no idea what he was saying, and I assumed he was praying in an unknown tongue. He then turned towards Dorcas, and calling her by her Hebrew name said, "Tabitha, get up."

That was it. That was the whole thing. Before my own eyes, Dorcas opened her eyes and looked around. Then her eyes opened even wider and she said, "You are Peter."

Peter said, "Yes, I know. I am Peter, and you dear lady are Dorcas—greatly loved by God and greatly loved by these people." Turning toward me he said, "Bring them in, brothers—no wait, there isn't room in here, let's take you out to them. Besides, I want you to get out of this room so I can stay here a few days." He smiled and I thought I would burst with happiness.

We opened the door to a large crowd on the roof of the house, and an even larger crowd outside below. First, James stepped out, then I did, and next came Peter leading Dorcas by the arm. The entire assembly of people gasped at the same time. After a moment of silence Peter said, "Brothers and sisters I am pleased to present to you, by the power of Jesus Christ and his resurrection from the dead, our sister Dorcas, also now risen from the dead."

Now every shred of silence for some distance was shattered by cheers and shouts and hallelujahs. It went on for two, three, five, ten, thirty minutes and more. It was as if the angels of God had joined us in cheering and shouting just like at the creation of the world. People jumped up and down while they shouted. Some danced. Others clapped each other on the arms and embraced. All shouted, cheered, and hugged and kissed Dorcas.

Dorcas was a joy to watch. At first she didn't realize that she had died and been raised again, but as the realization dawned on her, she joined in the cheering and shouting. We cheered and shouted until some of us fell on the ground gasping for breath. Gradually the celebration stopped, not because we wanted to stop, but because of exhaustion. I was certain that some of the heavenly beings had joined us during the celebration.

It was getting late and there were many people at the tannery. I had a perfect sized calf for a banquet, so we butchered the calf and started the fire while those who lived close enough went to their homes to get bread and raisin cakes. Several of them brought skins of wine, and we had a banquet that lasted far into the night.

The evening was perfect for our gathering. We felt that it was so because the Lord was there, and wanted to enjoy the banquet with us. We sang, danced and chatted. Then listened to Peter share the exciting things that had been happening everywhere the apostles had gone following the persecution. It was thrilling to hear those stories, and we all looked forward to the soon return of Jesus. We thought it had to be soon now, because of these things happening everywhere.

The banquet ended on a hilarious note. Peter had finished his report and a few others had commented. After a moment of silence, Dorcas said, "I'm so tired I could just die."

Every ounce of remaining energy was spent in laughter. We roared, and when the laughter finally began to subside Peter said, "That's it. Go home now. I can't take any more. Go home in the love and peace of God." People were still laughing and chuckling as they slowly went off towards Joppa.

Dorcas did die again three years later, but that time it was the real thing—or rather the time she was planted in the ground to await the resurrection of her body. Her presence during those three years was a powerful testimony to Jesus and his power over death.

Peter stayed on with us for a long time. He fell in love with the beauty of the surroundings, and the opportunities he had to spend time with the Lord. I encouraged him to stay on permanently, but though he might have wanted to, he did not. However, he sent for his wife and children, and for several months made Joppa his home.

The months spent with Peter and his family were rich and rewarding. This was due, not only to the many significant events that occurred, but also to every hour and minute we were able to share life with joy and a common purpose. Our lives belonged to Jesus, and he was with us in our talking, walking and making sandals. Looking back, I feel the significance of this passing remark Peter made during one of our many walks together along the beach: "I feel like something is about to break loose—like when Mary broke the jar of perfume. The perfume wasn't held in anymore, but filled the whole room."

CHAPTER TWENTY

JOPPA

Peter and Hannah were like raisin cakes at a banquet. Our life at Joppa was already rich and full, blessed beyond anything we could have imagined. When Peter and Hannah joined us it became even better. The community was happy and fulfilled, and we also felt secure and solid. We knew we belonged to a loved people that spanned our nation, and even heaven and earth. We were part of the family of God, and we felt the greatness of that family.

Peter, a great apostle, prayed often. Although he was up praying at all hours of the day or night, his prayer life was not mere religious observation. Peter and the Lord were friends and Peter talked with the Lord as much as he did with those around him. When he prayed with some of us, it was respectful and humble, but I felt I could look around and the Lord would be present just like the rest of us.

This great apostle also laughed a lot. He would burst into joyous laughter spontaneously and infectiously. No matter who you were, in terms of position and class, when you were with Peter you recognized his greatness, and his genuine friendship toward you. He was like an old fishing companion that accepted you completely, and did not put on any kind of shield or protective image. When he was with you, he was wholly with you. You were important and respected, whether you were an elder in the community, or the child of a slave.

He loved to walk along the beach. If you wanted to find Peter and didn't know where he was, you first looked on the roof where he often prayed. If he wasn't there, your next choice was to check along the beach.

I spent as much time with Peter as possible. I often suggested walks on the beach with him, or slowed down the progress as much as possible on the sandals I was making for him while he was waiting. Sometimes, when a brother came to me for counsel and Peter was there, I would try to draw Peter into the conversation, and to defer to him as the leader and spiritual authority. Peter would not allow me to do that. Once, after my typically unsuccessful attempt to thrust him into a contrived relationship with a new brother, Peter corrected me.

Later, when we were alone, Peter said, "Malchus, I feel you're trying to mold me into an unreal office, into some kind of high priest or man with all the answers. You talk to the same Lord I do. The Lord Jesus drew that beautiful young brother into this community, and into your care, so you could disciple him and help him grow into a mature man of God. Do it, and don't cheat yourself out of the blessing of watching him grow up in the Lord.

"Jesus equipped you to do the work," Peter continued. "And after a couple of years, or however long it will take to bring the young man to mature, spirit-empowered service to the Lord. Let him stand with the Lord Jesus. If he continues to come to you, ignore him, disregard him, or talk to him like I'm talking to you.

"Your goal is to work yourself out of the job of discipling a person. See that his relationship to Jesus and the community is strong and clear, then get out of the way. If he needs you, you're around. But if he comes to you to do his praying, take his responsibilities, or do his work, then rebuke him. Don't let others put you in the place of the Lord.

"Remember," Peter warned me sternly, "that the Lord is merciful and gracious, but he is also jealous, and the people— you and me—we people, are his people.

"Also brother," he continued, "you are an elder of the Church of Joppa. You sit at the gates and together with the other elders, you govern this city through the church in behalf of the Lord Jesus. Maybe it's better to say that the Lord Jesus governs this city through you, his elders, who are the governors of his precious and holy people. However you say it Malchus, or Simon, there is no higher office than the one you hold.

"As an apostle I am set first in the church, but when I come to the Church of Joppa, I come through the gates that the Lord has established. You, and James and the other elders sit at those gates and say what can come in and out. I am here because, now that the Church is here, you invited me through those gates and I, your fellow Elder, came through the gates you opened. Do you understand what I'm saying?"

"Yes I do," I answered, "and I receive your correction about putting myself down, or putting you up in a wrong place. Thank you, Peter."

We had walked some distance along the beach during this conversation. We turned back and were silent for a few minutes. I raised the issue of money and the treasure stash that continued to grow, thinking I could give it all to Peter. "While we're here and alone Peter, I'd like to take care of the issue of the money."

"What do you mean, 'the issue of the money?'" he asked.

"Well, you remember when I gave you the bag of money Bethany and I had saved; we were at Joanna's house. You took it, accepted it, and then gave it back to me to manage for the Lord?"

"Yes, I remember," Peter said. "So, what about it?"

"I would like to make an accounting of it, and give it back to you."

"My dear brother, I am not the Lord. I believe it was the Holy Spirit that moved you to give the money that day. I know it was the Holy Spirit who told me to accept it, and then give it back to you to manage for him. I am curious about it, but you manage it for him, not for me."

I looked a little puzzled since I had thought the community of believers at Jerusalem had everything in common, and that the Lord would probably lead us in that same direction. "You mean, you don't still have everything in common," I asked?

"No, we do not, and really never did hold everything in common," Peter replied. "The Lord moved among us, and those with extra houses or fields sold them and brought the money to us, so that no one was in need. It was wonderful, and we need to see everything we have as belonging to God and his family. So if something I have is needed by someone else, then I need to give it to the one in need.

"But some problems surfaced in Jerusalem regarding the money, and the responsibility of managing it for the Lord. One couple even worked out a scheme to lie to us about how much they sold a field for. They came with part of the money, and said it was the whole price. Can you believe that?"

"That's incredible," I responded! "What happened?"

"God killed them. He killed them one at a time. First the husband came in and told us, 'We sold the field for such and such.' The Spirit told me it was a lie, I told him so, and he fell over dead. The young men carried him out and buried him. His wife came in telling the same story, and she died also. The people became serious about being honest," Peter laughed.

Then he continued, "Taking care of each other became the official responsibility of the apostles. Pretty soon we were so busy, we had the people select some men to serve as deacons. Soon after that, Stephen was killed, as you know, and the persecution caused most of the believers to be spread all over the world. I understand that a few settlements of believers have tried to live communally with a common purse and all, but they are exceptions. There are some wonderful benefits of being part of a community like that, but there are also many problems, and unless God specifically says to do it, to live like that, I think we're better off with the type of relationships that I see here in Joppa."

"I think you're right, Peter," I said as we climbed the slope to the house.

I spent some time seeking God's desire about the money, and about Peter, and some of the needs of the poor in Jerusalem, now that so many of the believers were gone. I went up the steps, and sure enough, Peter was there on the roof, praying. "Here Peter," I said as I handed him a purse with a large sum of money. "This is one third of the money I am managing for God. At one point after we arrived here in Joppa, the money was only about half of what we started with. That was when we built the house and the tannery, and also sowed money into some of the brothers in need. But since then, it keeps growing and growing. The business is good, and the more I try to give it away, the more it comes back to me."

"Praise God," Peter exclaimed. "I receive it. Is there anything you want me to do with this?"

"Hey, brother," I poked at him. "The Holy Spirit said it was all right to give you one third of the money on hand. That's what I'm doing. Now you're stuck to manage it, so don't try to make me responsible for your job."

Peter's eyes grew extra wide, and he roared with laughter. At last he said, "If we go on with this eye for eye business, we'll both be blind before long." As he continued to laugh he bellowed, "That's good, Simon. That's really good."

* * *

A few weeks later, God opened our hearts and minds to another aspect of his will and desire. It was beautiful, and yet cut across the grain of our thinking and tradition. We were enjoying the favor of God upon our family of believers. Ever since the conversion of Saul, the persecution against us had diminished. We would have been happy to go on as we were for years, but God had other plans for his people.

Peter was up and gone from the house before the sun had risen. That was not unusual. I discovered he had gone down to the beach to pray, and had prayed right through the time we breakfasted. That was unusual—unless he was fasting—which he was not. It was late morning before he returned.

He went into the house to get some bread or something to eat. Bethany, Hannah, Sarah and the young servant girls, who were being discipled by Bethany, were just starting to bake. Soon after breakfast they had prayed and fellowshipped together, and by now they should have finished the baking.

Peter came boldly into the women's domain and asked, "Is there no bread, or something to eat for a starving man?"

Hannah put an arm around her husband. "A starving man is it? My dear husband, you could live for many a week on this pouch of food stored right here," Hannah retorted while playfully poking at the small but noticeable bulge around Peter's middle.

"I come for food, and I get insulted. What kind of hospitality is this?" Peter joked.

Bethany was not to be left out of the fun, nor did she appreciate any male intrusion into her area. "Shoo, scat, get out of here. Go and do great and wonderful things for God, but stay out of my kitchen." Then smiling she said, "I'll call you when the bread is ready."

From there Peter came to the shop where I was making some sandals for one of the girls. He knew I often had a little jerkied meat or some bread stashed away. "Simon," he greeted me, " do you have anything to eat? I am ravenously hungry and the women just sent me away, I know better than to press it with them, but I thought you might have something here."

"Sorry Peter. A young man came out just after breakfast for some prayer and counsel. He was hungry, so I gave him all I had here. You'll just have to fast whether you want to or not," I laughed. "Maybe Joseph or Jehoiada have something down at the tannery."

Peter replied, "No. Whenever I go down there I lose my appetite, and sometimes the food I've already eaten." He turned and went up the stairs to the roof.

All was quiet and still for about an hour. I was getting a bit hungry now also, so I left the shop to see what the women were doing. As I started towards the house I noticed three men approaching. Standing there to see who they might be, I began to panic as I realized they were Romans, in fact one of them was an officer. "Lord, have mercy on us. Protect us by your grace."

When they reached the gate they stopped and called to me, "Is Simon, the one called Peter, staying here?"

Before I could answer Peter spoke up as he came down the stairs. "I'm the one you're looking for. Why have you come?" He looked shocked, like a person who had just experienced the death of a loved one.

The men replied, "We have come from Cornelius the centurion. He is a righteous and God-fearing man, who is respected by all the Jewish people. A holy angel told him to

159

have you come to his house so that he could hear what you have to say."

Peter responded, "Come in. Come in."

It was not unusual for us to have houseguests. But these three were gentiles! That had never happened. The tension throughout the household was like heavy clouds in a storm with lightning flashing back and forth. We were all strained and the muscles in our bodies were tight.

Jehoiada, Joseph and the other workers came straight from the tannery without first washing in the sea. The smell was bad. We set up the benches and put the small tables together with our large one as we often did when guests were present. It was difficult for the women to move between the tables. The silence was intense as we stood still by our places waiting for Peter to say something. No one moved, yet every set of eyes darted back and forth as in a frenzied search.

Peter took the bread, broke it, and blessed it. I felt violated. Gentiles in my house . . . eating my food . . . sitting at my table . . . defiling my family. The gentiles were waiting for us to eat, and we were waiting for something. The silence was heavy.

Peter took a few bites of bread and spoke at last. He said, "I was extremely hungry this noon, and while this meal was being prepared, I went up to the roof to pray. I fell into a trance. I saw heaven opened and something like a large sheet being let down to earth by its four corners. It contained all kinds of four-footed animals, as well as reptiles of the earth and birds of the air. Then a voice told me, 'Rise, Peter. Kill and eat.'

"I replied, 'Surely not, Lord! I have never eaten anything impure or unclean.'

"The voice spoke to me a second time, 'Do not call anything impure that God has made clean.'

"This happened three times, and immediately the sheet was taken back to heaven.

Peter continued, "While I was wondering about the meaning of this vision, these men from Cornelius were walking up the path to this house. I was thinking about it and the Spirit said to me, 'Simon, three men are looking for you. So get up and go downstairs. Do not hesitate to go with them, for I have sent them.' This is what happened, and now I would like to eat something."

I spoke up and said, "God is breaking centuries of tradition within us. I feel like a war is being fought inside me." Then, addressing the gentiles, I continued, "It is hard to open our home to you gentiles, but in the light of what is happening I say to you—you are welcome here. Please be patient with our hesitating to be hospitable. It is hard to break the tradition of our father's fathers."

Gradually the tension eased. The three became less gentiles and more men in our eyes. I observed that our young ones easily accepted these men as people, but we, older ones, had to struggle to stay open to the work of God in our midst.

After the meal, Peter asked to meet with me, and requested that I send Joseph to fetch James and any other leaders who could come. He said to tell them that we would be praying and counseling together about going to Caesarea, and that they should make the trip with us if possible. If any of them could not afford the time away from their work, we would give them what financial help was necessary.

After Joseph had left, I said, "Peter, you said, 'make the trip with us.' Have you forgotten about Caiaphas and the reward he has offered for my arrest?"

"No, I haven't forgotten, Peter answered. "But this is so important, so critical in the faith, that I want you with me. It is a crowded road between Joppa and Caesarea, and you can stay in the midst of the brothers. Also, once arrived, no Jews will be there to see you in the home of a gentile. I want you to come my friend, but if you feel in God that you cannot or should not, I will understand."

It would be a couple hours before the brothers began arriving. I decided to go for a long walk on the beach so I could have some time alone, in communion with God. For seven years I had been isolated on this piece of property, except for evening visits to the sick in Joppa. Although Caiaphas had stepped down as High Priest, his sons were following in his footsteps, and the danger was still real. "Lord, may I go to Caesarea? Should I go? I would like to be there to see if somehow the message of Jesus is to go beyond us Jewish believers. How do I tell Bethany? Help, Lord, give me wisdom!"

CHAPTER TWENTY-ONE

JOPPA

Peter was sensing the significance of the trip to Caesarea and the meeting with Cornelius. If God should reach out to this Roman centurion, this gentile, centuries of tradition would be shattered. Even our understanding of Jesus and the way we relate to God would be adjusted. Reaching out to gentiles was a radical departure. Saul had talked about it when he was with us, but it had never been done.

Peter wanted as many of us as possible to go with him. He was committed to following the Lord, but his mind was still reeling from the vision he had seen. His entire lifetime of following the practices of traditional Jewish culture were challenged, and Peter knew from experience that when he and the Lord conflicted, God always won. Peter wanted moral support, if nothing else.

The evening after the brothers had arrived, we decided that I should go to Caesarea, as well as James, Joseph and three others. Since Jehoiada was now fifteen, I decided to take him along, and Peter concurred. That night, we spent a long time in prayer, asking the Lord to prepare us for this encounter, and to keep our hearts open and sensitive to the Spirit. This was a traumatic time.

Since some of the men had to make arrangements before leaving for a few days, we planned to meet together at James' house at noon the next day, and leave for Caesarea from there. Our group, ten men and a Roman officer, was different from those usually seen on the road. No one bothered us, and when people did look our way, I noticed they focused their attention

163

on the Roman officer. My fears of detection and arrest were unfounded.

The following day, we arrived at Caesarea. Cornelius was expecting us, and had called together his relatives and close friends. As Peter entered the house, Cornelius met him and fell at his feet in reverence. But Peter made him get up. "Stand up," he said, "I am only a man myself."

Talking with him, Peter went inside and found a large gathering of people. He said to them, "You are well aware that it is against our law for a Jew to associate with a gentile or visit him. But God has shown me that I should not call any man impure or unclean, so I came without raising any objections. May I ask why you sent for me?"

Cornelius answered, "Four days ago I was in my house praying at this hour, at three o'clock in the afternoon. Suddenly, a man in shining clothes stood before me and said, 'Cornelius, God has heard your prayer and remembered your gifts to the poor. Send to Joppa for Simon who is called Peter. He is a guest in the home of Simon the tanner, who lives by the sea.' So I sent for you immediately, and it was good of you to come. Now we are all here in the presence of God to listen to everything the Lord has commanded you to tell us."

Peter began to speak: "I now realize how true it is that God does not show favoritism but, from every nation, accepts men who fear him and do what is right. This is the message God sent to the people of Israel, telling the good news of peace through Jesus Christ, who is Lord of all. You know what happened in Galilee after the baptism that John had preached—how God anointed Jesus of Nazareth with the Holy Spirit and power, and how Jesus went around performing good deeds and healing all who were under the power of the devil, because God was with him.

"We are witnesses of everything he did in the country of the Jews and in Jerusalem. They killed him by hanging him on a tree, but God raised him from the dead on the third day and caused him to be seen. He was not seen by all the people, but by witnesses whom God had already chosen—by us who ate and drank with him after he rose from the dead. He commanded us to preach to the people and to testify that he is the one whom

164

God appointed as judge of the living and the dead. All the prophets testify about him, that everyone who believes in him, receives forgiveness of sins through his name."

While Peter was still speaking these words, the Holy Spirit came on all who had heard the message. We, Jewish believers who came with Peter, were astonished that the gift of the Holy Spirit had been poured out even on the gentiles. We knew this had happened for we heard them speaking in tongues and praising God.

Peter then said to us, "Can anyone keep these people from being baptized with water? They have received the Holy Spirit just as we have." We were stunned at the work of God among these gentiles, and we nodded our agreement with Peter, concerning water baptism. Peter ordered that they be baptized in the name of Jesus Christ.

We did the baptizing there, in Cornelius' house in a large Roman bath which easily accommodated James, myself and the person being baptized. Cornelius, his family and friends entered the bath at one end, James and I baptized them, and as they left the bath at the other end, the next candidate took their place. Peter stood at the edge of the bath explaining the meaning of baptism.

He said that the water is like the flood in Noah's day. The flood killed and drowned all the corrupted world, yet it also saved Noah and his family from the destruction. The water is both death and life. It is death to the world with Jesus, and life with Jesus through his resurrection.

When the new believers had all been baptized, we prayed for each one. We did not all pray for one person at the same time, but each of us prayed for a new believer. This praying and ministering went on for an hour or more. Some of the new believers were healed of sickness and deformity, from others demons fled with their obnoxious shrieks and smells, and most of the new flock received prophetic messages from those of us with the gift of prophecy.

As the time of ministry continued, the wall that separated us as Jew and Gentile was destroyed. We were so happy being used by God, as his instruments, and these gentiles were so happy at receiving the grace of God, that the wall just disappeared. However, the wall reappeared when Cornelius presented a banquet later that evening.

Cornelius was sensitive to the Jewish laws, so no unclean foods were served, but the tradition which forbids Jews eating with Gentiles rebuilt the wall anew. We had to fight consciously against our ingrained tradition and religion for the sake of Jesus and his body of believers. These gentiles were part of God's close family now, and so we became close family too.

Cornelius asked that Peter stay with them for a few days to teach them more about Jesus. In the morning, it was decided that Peter and James would both stay in Caesarea to share their knowledge and experience with Cornelius and his congregation of believers. The rest of us would return that day to Joppa. From there, Joseph was to go directly to Jerusalem to notify the other apostles, and to ask them to send some of the apostles to Cornelius' house, especially James, the Lord's brother, and John if they were available.

We left about noon and made good time approaching Apollonia about sunset. This was well over half way and we were getting tired. We all expected to stay at a khan near the village, get a fresh start in the morning and be home before noon. As we drew near the khan, a mounted contingent of Roman soldiers, Temple guards and others, approached from the south. We stepped back out of the way to let them pass, but they turned and went into the khan just ahead of us. I tried to stay behind the others, but did not want to be conspicuous by my shrinking from sight.

Although they paid no attention to us, I was stunned. It felt like my stomach had gone up into my throat and was choking me. Meraioth, the contemptuous man who took my place with Caiaphas, was in the group, and several of the guards looked familiar. I began trembling while some of the brothers were complaining that this group might take all the available sleeping space in the khan. Joseph noticed my distress and asked, "Simon, what's wrong?"

"I know some of those men, and they must not see me," I replied.

The others with me looked confused, but one of them just said, "Well, we'll go on then."

166

"No brothers," I replied, "you stay here as we had planned. It might seem strange if we all went on at this point. Please don't make more of this, or react strangely towards those men in there, or you may arouse suspicion. If God wills, I will give you an explanation at some other time, but please just stay here and act as normally as possible. Jehoiada and I will press on for Joppa and home. Pray for us for a safe trip and an absence of robbers."

Turning, I took hold of Jehoiada's arm, and we left quickly so as not to draw attention. "Well son, I hope you're up to a long day, and a tiring journey." Glancing upward I added, "And Lord, let your angels attend us and keep us from all danger and evil on this road."

I put an arm around Jehoiada's broadening shoulders and smiled. He leaned in closer to me and smiling back said, "I am glad I got to go on this journey with you, Father. I like being with you, and with the other men too. I don't think anyone from that group of soldiers and guards recognized you, do you?"

"No, I don't think so either, but it was a fright to see Meraioth and those guards with him."

"Who is he, Father? Did you know him well?" Jehoiada asked.

"I was his overseer in Caiaphas' service. When I disappeared after Jesus was crucified, he took over many of my jobs and also treated me badly when I returned to see Caiaphas. He is the kind of man who carries a grudge for a long time, and would probably still like to hurt me. I imagine he is in the service of Theophilus, one of Caiaphas' sons who is the present High Priest."

Jehoiada and I walked briskly and talked for two or three hours about the things that had happened during the time of Jesus' betrayal and crucifixion. He had some misconceptions, and was full of questions. When the conversation began to lag, he looked at me and said, "I'm glad you're my father."

I responded as best I could, "You are a fine son, and a precious gift from God. I am not worthy of you Jehoiada, but I also am glad that you are my son."

Fatigue began to take its toll on our conversation. We walked on in silence for two more hours, arriving in Joppa after midnight. We considered staying at the home of one of the brothers, but decided we could make it home in the same time it would take to wake someone and get settled. We pushed on the short distance to our beloved home, where I promised myself I would not leave. I kept the promise for almost ten years.

Bethany woke up at our arrival and wanted to feed us and hear all about the adventure. With the vigor of youth and the insatiable appetite of a fifteen-year-old Jehoiada quickly revived. My bodily systems, however, were assuring me there was no danger, I was safe and now was the time for rest. After nodding a time or two while Bethany prepared the meal and listened to Jehoiada's animated account of the last three days, I said, "I love you and look forward to talking tomorrow, but I must go to bed, I'm exhausted."

Bethany started to make a joke about this, but when she looked at me she just said, "I understand. Welcome home, my lord Malchus. I thank God for your safe return."

The next day Bethany and I were both tired. She had listened to Jehoiada for two hours and then lay awake most of the night pondering the things he had shared. Not just the things he shared, but the man who shared them. She was impressed with her son. He had officially become a man a few years back, but she realized that night that Jehoiada was interesting, perceptive and had much understanding. He was a delightful young man.

She was grateful for her revelation of the manhood of Jehoiada, and she tried to be grateful for the revelation that the faith of Jesus was now going beyond the Jewish people to all the gentiles. She knew it was right, but the breaking of the old tradition was painful and difficult. She spent most of the night praying that the followers of the Way would survive this transition, no matter how hard it was.

An uproar ensued, once the word about Cornelius and the gentiles reached the apostles in Jerusalem, then the brothers scattered throughout Judea. Peter had barely returned to Joppa, when messengers arrived from Jerusalem asking him to come and explain why he had done this. Again, Peter requested that the brothers who had accompanied him to Caesarea also come to Jerusalem, including Jehoiada, but excluding me.

They were gone for several days, and returned rejoicing in God and strengthened in our growing understanding that the good news about Jesus would spread throughout the earth to every nation and people. Joseph was sent by Peter to several of the communities in Judea to report what happened at Caesarea and at the meeting in Jerusalem. Jehoiada brought the report to our portion of the Church of Joppa that met at the tannery.

We were all eager to hear first hand about Jerusalem, but I was especially excited about hearing the report from Jehoiada. Bethany and I felt he was called to be a leader in the church, and I wanted to determine if this was parental hopefulness or the anointing of God. After some small talk about the trip, Jehoiada said, "The meeting was in an upper room assembly hall with about a hundred people. There was shouting and arguing and tremendous noise and confusion. As we arrived certain people began rebuking us, even me. But Peter really was chastised. He was surrounded by angry brothers who said he never should have gone into the house of an uncircumcised man and eaten with him.

"At this point Peter raised his arms for silence, and although it was slow in coming, it finally grew quiet. Peter told the story exactly like it happened starting with his vision here on the roof, the visit to Cornelius' house and the outpouring of the Holy Spirit upon those gentiles. He shrugged his shoulders, put his palms up and said something like, 'So brothers, what could I do? The Lord gave his Spirit to them. I asked the brothers with me if we could refuse them baptism, but they agreed we couldn't, so we baptized them. Who was I to think I could oppose God?'

"When the brothers heard the whole story, they stopped being critical, but some of them seemed to pout. What I sensed was that some were saying, 'Well I don't like this, but if it was God doing it, I suppose I have to go along.'"

We all laughed at Jehoiada's interpretation of these brothers. It helped, since we felt like that too. Then my son continued with a powerful exhortation: "Brothers and sisters, we need to know the ways of God. God said much about the Gentiles through the prophets of old, but we did not, or chose not to, understand what God meant when Isaiah said that Jesus was 'a light to lighten the gentiles, and the glory of his people Israel.' We need to know the ways of God.

"We also need to fit into the ways of God. It is difficult for us to embrace the gentiles the way the Holy Spirit is embracing them, but we need to do it. We must! We need to know the ways of God, and then to fit into the ways of God.

"But even more than this, brothers and sisters, we need to learn to love the ways of God. If Jesus loves the gentiles, I need to love them also, and love the idea of loving them, simply because it is God's way. We need to know the ways of God; fit into the ways of God; and we need to love the ways of God."

When Jehoiada finished, the congregation applauded. They applauded not only because he was one of their own, but also because of the powerful truth he spoke and the conviction the Holy Spirit mixed with his words. I was unable to continue the meeting for some time.

CHAPTER TWENTY-TWO

ROME

Wide awake, yet not present in my surroundings in the Roman prison, I am brought back to reality by a gentle shaking from Cleomus. What is this transformation of Cleomus? A gentle shaking? "Malchus, I think you should know that some friend of yours has received permission to see you before you make your decision in the morning. I was told he was your friend, but I doubt he's coming to encourage you."

"Do you know his name, Cleomus?" I ask.

"Demas."

"Demas?"

"Yes, Demas. Do you know him well?" Cleomus asks.

"Yes I do," I reply. "He is from Pisidia, somewhere between Antioch and Iconium. He was an early convert to the faith when Saul of Tarsus began travelling through the regions preaching about Jesus and his resurrection. Many people received the message and became followers of the Way, but there was trouble and even some serious persecutions, especially from the Jews in the area."

"You Christians manage to stir up trouble everywhere," Cleomus comments.

"I think it comes at us, Cleomus, because we proclaim that Jesus is the Lord and rightful ruler of all things. He rose from the dead and laid claim to all people, and the Devil doesn't like it. Satan doesn't want to give up his domain, and he pretty well rules everything through his specialties of lying, cheating, killing and destroying."

"I don't believe in the Devil," Cleomus snaps back with a little of his old hostility.

"I didn't either," I simply state. "Anyway, Demas began to travel with Saul, or now Paul as he is known, and that summer they headed for Jerusalem to meet with the apostles there and report what was happening."

"Who are apostles?" Cleomus asks.

"Apostles are the ones who were with Jesus and who saw him after he rose from the dead. There are some others, like Paul who also saw Jesus. The word 'apostle' means someone who is sent, and the apostles are the ones Jesus is sending today to proclaim his truth and establish churches."

"All right," Cleomus interrupts, "how did you meet this Demas?"

"It was six or seven years ago, when Paul, Demas and some others headed for Jerusalem. Demas became sick on the ship which made port at Joppa. They all came to my place to spend the night, and in the morning Demas had to stay with us. On their way back about a week later, he was still too sick to travel, so he spent several months with us."

"My wife Bethany is a good servant to the sick. She spends considerable time praying, has plenty of patience and encourages people; so she helped Demas regain his health—it's really hard to talk about her or to think about her, Cleomus. I miss her so much. God willing some day you may meet her.

"Anyway, Demas was like part of the family during those months, and we spent a good deal of time together. He wasn't strong enough to work in our tannery, so he mostly stayed around me in the shop while I made sandals. When other brothers would come to me for counsel or prayer, Demas would join in with us. He'd get excited and animated about the need to go throughout the world with the message. One of his favorite sayings was, 'We have to get the message to everybody before Jesus comes back.'"

"If you were a wagering man, I'd wager he doesn't feel like that now," Cleomus said.

"Why do you say that?"

"Use your head, Malchus," Cleomus retorts. "If he was so inspired to tell everybody about Jesus, why would the centurion let him come see you? He had to get permission to come here, and not many are granted such a visit. What do you think he wants to tell you? The centurion must have asked him. If he said he wanted to encourage you to die like a man, he wouldn't be coming. And, not many people would be foolish enough to lie to the centurion."

"This really upsets me, Cleomus. You must be right, but I hate the thought of it. I love Demas, and so does my family. I hope it isn't so."

"For your sake, I hope so too, Malchus, but you'd be wise to be prepared for the worst," Cleomus counseled. "I must go and tend to some other duties."

Alone again I keep repeating, "Demas, Demas, Demas." At last I pray. I pray for Bethany that if Demas has defected from the faith, she won't be devastated when she finds out. I pray for Cleomus, and ask the Holy Spirit to keep up the work he is doing in Cleomus. I pray for myself and the next hours of imprisonment and then the encounter with death or betrayal. I ask the Lord about Demas and how I should pray for him. I hear, or sense in my spirit, to think about the days when Demas was with us in Joppa. Obediently, my thoughts race back to Joppa.

JOPPA

Jehoiada was a man of twenty-one. He ran the tannery better than I, he taught and exhorted the people better than I, he bartered with merchants and shippers better than I. My only complaint was that he was not married. We spoke of it often, and I threatened to make some arrangements, but he always said, "God will provide my wife and make it clear if I am to marry. Otherwise, I will serve him and his people as a eunuch."

He was right in his attitude, but I yearned for children's children, and though Sarah wanted to marry, the right young man was not obvious, and besides, she was too young. Bethany and I thought that anyone younger than we had been was too young.

Our way of life at the tannery had remained much the same over the years, but on a larger scale. More and more brothers stayed with us on their travels since Joppa was an active port, though not as busy as Caesarea. We had built a guest house when Peter and Hannah stayed so long with us, and then expanded it over the years.

Demas fit right in with the constant activity. Wherever something was happening, Demas was in the middle of it. If several men were working at the tannery, Demas would be hanging around talking about the Lord's work. When I had brothers in the shop, Demas would sit with us to watch me work and to join in the conversations. When Bethany, Sarah and the women were busy with baking or sewing, Demas would be in the middle of it talking and laughing with them as he watched them work.

When the revelation came to me, it was like a cart load of skins falling on top of me: Demas never worked. He talked, and told about what he had done, but he never did anything. I know he was sick for a long time, but he could have done something, I mused. He could have handed Jehoiada, or others in the tannery, a shovel, or the knife, or moved a skin, but he only talked. He could have handed me needles, or thongs, or pieces of leather, but he was a talker, not a helper. He could have done many things for Bethany, but he only talked. Demas did not work.

I began to recall specific conversations when Demas would vigorously exhort us to be more forceful in telling others about Jesus. I had thought that my discomfort came from a conviction that I wasn't doing all I could do for the Kingdom of God and so I felt guilty. I was beginning to see something else. Bethany one time said to me, "When Demas is talking to me, especially when he gets so excited about taking the message to others, I feel like he is talking to me with his mind and thoughts, but his heart and his soul are a couple of cubits behind somewhere." At the time it made no sense, but now it was clear: Demas had no peace. He was driven to say things that sounded right and were supposed to stir people to action, but it did not come from peace, and therefore imparted anxiety and strife. This was my second revelation.

I say out loud, "Lord, if these revelations are correct, why didn't you tell us then?"

The response I hear, or sense, contains a tinge of anger. "No one sought me about it, and no one asked."

After I apologize and ask the Lord to forgive me, more episodes come to mind. Two of the brothers who worked at the port were telling us about some slaves with whom they worked. They had an opportunity, over the noon meal, to talk with them about Jesus, and one of them showed a genuine interest. We were discussing how the brothers might follow up on this opportunity when Demas broke in and chided us all. "Don't worry about the slaves, get to their master. If you can win the master, the slaves will follow along and become believers too." He was right, but why did it seem so wrong?

A similar situation arose with some soldiers. Demas argued that the first priority should be to reach the officers and leaders. Then all would follow. It was sound logic. It was a strategic approach. It was impeccable, but the realization hit me again: it was centered in and responsive to man, instead of being responsive to the Lord. It was man directed instead of God directed. It was seeking approval of men, not approval of God. It was direction by human wisdom instead of direction by divine wisdom, or the mind of Messiah.

I feel foolish that as a leader I did not recognize these things when Demas was with us. I didn't recognize his preference of the rich over the poor for what it was; or his keen interest in people who seemed important, and his lack of time for the lesser ones. As I start to berate myself and call myself stupid, I hear a voice loud and strong within me, "Stop this. I am pleased with you my son, and I do not want you to be so harsh on one whom I love."

Grateful for his intervention I respond, "Thank you Father."

ROME

Cleomus again comes in and sits on my mat. He doesn't say anything, but just sits there. I begin with, "I've been thinking about Demas, and I have realized some things I didn't put together then. I'm afraid you're right about him, Cleomus."

Cleomus just shakes his head.

I continue, "Even though I see some things about him, I still love him, and I am looking forward to seeing him."

"I'll never understand you crazy Christians," Cleomus mutters. "You love those who are your enemies, and do good to rotten people."

I sense that Cleomus is not talking about Demas, but himself. "Cleomus, I hope some day you will understand. We have all been rotten people, yet God gave his own son for us. I hope the love of God will fill you up, and spill out of you to others." Silence. I continue, "I am grateful to God that I got to know you a little bit. I wish it had been in a different place and time, but I count you as a friend. God bless you, Cleomus."

He sits for just an instant with his mouth slightly open, then rises and walks out.

"Lord," I pray, "adopt him as your son, instruct him as your disciple, and love him as your friend." A deep peace again seems to envelope me and I return my thoughts to the last days in Joppa.

JOPPA

A few years after Demas had left us, Peter informed me that Caiaphas, now an old man, was ill and not expected to live. There was trouble between the Romans and the Jews; Emperor Claudius had banished the Jews from Rome, but they were already filtering back in. Rome still appointed the High Priest, so there was some cooperation here in Israel, but the tension was growing. Caiaphas' third son, Matthias was now the High Priest, and my old rival Meraioth was his chief assistant.

Jehoiada was still single, and Sarah, now approaching eighteen, was interested in a young man in Joppa. Bethany and

I were praying about him and the possibility of a wedding, but we weren't settled in our hearts yet.

Joseph returned from his ministry travels each year and stayed for a month or until he had a new assignment. He would go with another brother to a certain community in Israel and stay for a year or less. He helped train leaders, taught in meetings from house to house, and served as an example of the Lord Jesus. The apostles asked that these ministry teams not stay beyond one year lest the family of God begin to rely on "outside experts" and stifle the leadership that God was raising up in the midst of his people.

Bethany was called upon often to care for the sick, help with a family with special problems, or see that the poor were taken care of. She often made sure that orphaned children and the elderly were looked after in the absence of immediate family who could meet their needs. Since Dorcas' death, Bethany had taken her place.

I still counseled and prayed with others, but not as often as I used to, since many of the brothers were doing this as well. At the Sabbath meetings I was still looked to as the head, but the real work was done by Jehoiada and other younger leaders. I was happy and fulfilled in the meetings, but the desire to be used more by God grew stronger and caused me to pray often, "Lord, spend me as coin in your hand to accomplish your purposes on the earth."

My discontent grew stronger over the weeks and months, and I decided to stop being a self-imposed prisoner on my own property. I told Bethany that I was going to begin going to Joppa with Jehoiada and help him with the selling and loading of skins. She said, "I'll worry about you, but I know it's right for you to venture out. You used to go all over the country, and now for all these years you've been rooted here at this place."

"I've been happier and more blessed than anyone has the right to expect," I said. "But now I'm getting restless. I don't know if it's something God has for me to do, or if I'm just feeling unnecessary here. In truth, I am unnecessary. Everything would be just as fine without me as it is with me."

Sliding her arms around my middle Bethany said, "No, my lord. I would never be as fine without you as I am with you."

I smiled and held her silently and lovingly for several moments. Her love and devotion to me was sweet and precious, but her words did not ring true. Oh, I was certain they were true in her own heart, but I realized that she, like the rest of the family, could get along fine without me.

My first trip to Joppa with Jehoiada was to meet with an agent who was purchasing skins for a large supplier in Rome. We brought only a few samples, which Jehoiada carried over one shoulder. As we walked I reminisced our walk from Caesarea several years before. "This reminds me of the time we returned from Caesarea and walked the last part alone. That was a blessed time for me, Jehoiada."

"It was for me too, Father," Jehoiada said. "I treasure all the time we are together, but that time was special. I am glad we may get to go together again."

We had not gone far when Jehoiada said, "We have to turn off the road here so we don't go near the place the tax collectors stop those going in to Joppa. Otherwise we have to pay for the skins going in and coming out, as well as the time we sell them. I don't mind too much paying the taxes when we sell the skins, but I hate it when they make me pay for them two or three times."

"I don't blame you, I too would hate to pay it two or three times," I said.

Jehoiada stopped and looked at me. He said, "These skins belong to the Tannery of Simon. They are yours. You are the one who would have to pay two or three times."

I laughed and said, "I quickly forget that, son, since you take such good care of everything. Thank you."

He put his free arm around my shoulder and said, "Come on."

We went through a small gorge to the beach where a narrow path allowed us to walk on the cliff just above the water. Jehoiada said, "When the tide is out, you can walk along a sandy portion, but this is fine also."

It was fine for Jehoiada, but I was nervous walking on the edge of the rocks like this. In a few minutes, however, we arrived at the southern part of Joppa right at the port. We proceeded to a type of khan or inn at the port, where men, like the agent we were to meet, could stay and buy meals, and have a place to meet with their business associates.

The agent had just finished his meal when we arrived and joined him at his table. The business transaction was an education for me.

After Jehoiada introduced me as Simon, the agent said, "Oh, good. Now this son of yours doesn't have to put me off with his constant excuse, 'I must go and see if my father approves of this price.' I think he uses that as a lever to get the best possible price, and now we can deal directly."

"No, no!" I exclaimed. "He is the one you must deal with. If we did the business, I would have to go and get his approval."

The agent looked a little perplexed and Jehoiada broke right in with, "It won't be a problem. These are the samples of the skins, some of the best we have ever had, and we are willing to provide them for the same price as the last time. How many do you want?"

"Wait! Wait! Wait!" The agent exclaimed. "Last time we paid you the highest price ever. If we continue to pay such a price, we will lose money. We cannot continue like this. Besides we want 500 skins, and you must be able to lower the price significantly for such an order. Also, can you handle such an order?"

Jehoiada responded in a casual manner that shocked me. "Of course we can handle 500 skins. It's no problem for us, but we want the same price."

"No, no! We can't possibly pay that much for them. All dealers give a discount for larger volume. We will give you three fourths of the previous price for five hundred skins of this quality, delivered here to the ship Luxor in three weeks' time."

Jehoiada said, "We will deliver five hundred skins of this quality in three weeks to the Luxor, and take one twentieth off the price for the larger volume."

Back and forth they went for about half an hour. They walked about, shook their arms and fists, screamed and shouted, and finally agreed to take one ninth off the previous price. When it was all done, they shook hands and the agent said, "Agreed, my friend. I will send word when I am in the area again. It is good doing business with you."

"And with you my friend. Shalom until then," Jehoiada responded.

When we left, I had many questions. Where will you get five hundred skins? Can you make a profit at that price? How does he make payment?

Jehoiada laughed and said, "Father, we made an excellent deal. We have over three hundred skins at the tannery, and I can easily get another two hundred from other tanners at a price well under the amount he is paying us. We make money, not only on the skins we process, but on those of our countrymen as well. It is a good business. You can come again when we deliver them to the Luxor and see how it takes place."

Three weeks later, the skins were delivered to the Luxor, and I was delivered into the hand of God.

CHAPTER TWENTY-THREE

JOPPA

The Luxor arrived three days early, and was scheduled to remain in port for a week. Jehoiada had already bundled the three hundred skins from our tannery, covered them with a fine coating of damp clay and let them dry in the sun. This clay was easily cleaned once the skins reached their destination, and it absorbed moisture during shipping, to deter mildew and rot. The other two hundred skins were on hand and in various stages of readiness for shipment. Jehoiada said that with two days of sunshine, we would be in good shape. But, if we didn't get the two days of sunshine, we would load the untreated skins in the middle of the treated bundles with no problem.

Jehoiada and I went to the Luxor the day after she arrived to examine the cargo areas and find out when we could load. I enjoyed this adventure, as I had the previous outing when we met with the agent. The ship was a beauty, and Jehoiada was pleased with her storage places except for one that was exceptionally damp. He noted this to the captain and asked that we not be assigned that area—any other place would be good. We agreed, and loading was scheduled for the day after Sabbath, four days hence.

From the ship we went to old Bortheus' house, our grand friend who had originally sold us the tent so many years ago. He was over ninety years old, yet no specific ailment troubled him. He liked to say, "Old age caught me, and then ran over me like a runaway cart." Some days he felt fine and walked about the area near his house, but more and more he ceased venturing out. It was good to see him and pray together and reminisce on old times. Jehoiada enjoyed it also. I noticed his worn out sandals tied to his feet with a cord.

"Bortheus," I cried, "you must have some new sandals. I'll make them for you right away."

"Oh Simon, no. These will last my old bones till they plant me in the ground. Make the sandals for someone with more use of them. Besides, I don't want to pay good money for something that I won't wear out."

"Good. Then I won't have to refuse the money. I'll think about forgetting it, but in the meantime, I'll just measure these feet and see what size might feel good on them." I got down and quickly measured his feet. I didn't have any tools or leather with me to mark his foot, so I put his bony foot on my leg, just above the knee and used my fingernail to scratch the outline on my dry skin. I thought it would be visible for a long time, and when I got back to the shop I would cut out the pattern. If the line disappeared, I could remember close enough from the feel of his foot.

As we walked towards home Jehoiada said, "Let me see if I have figured you out. You are planning on going home and making some of the finest sandals possible for old Bortheus. Right?"

"Absolutely!" I answered. "It is a rare opportunity to do something neither practical nor expected for a good friend and brother, and is, therefore, an opportunity to give a most precious gift. We don't get many chances to do things like this," I said to Jehoiada.

"I seem to recall several chances that you have taken," he answered. "You know what this reminds me of?"

"No, what?" I asked.

"When Mary put the expensive perfume on Jesus' feet."

"Hmm," I responded. "It is something like that. The Lord Jesus is in Bortheus, and in a sense I'm doing it for him as well as Bortheus. But, I'd like to stop talking about it. I'm getting a little uncomfortable, and I don't want to loose the blessing or my happiness from giving this to Bortheus."

"I understand," Jehoiada said as we reached the property, and went in different directions. I headed straight for the shop looking to make certain the outline was still etched in my leg.

For the next two days, I labored over the sandals for Bortheus. I could have made the sandals themselves in half the time, but I spent considerable time decorating them, and even etching a design in the leather. I was extremely happy with them and when I finished I showed them to Bethany.

"Oh, Simon, they're beautiful," she said. "What a good friend you are! Now, after you give these to Bortheus, there is another family in Joppa who needs everything, including sandals. Maybe you could make some for them too?"

"Of course, I'll be happy to make sandals for them," I said feeling important and needed. "After Sabbath, I'll help Jehoiada and the others with the loading of the skins, visit Bortheus, then go see what we can do for this family."

* * *

In the morning we loaded our two carts to overflowing with thirty of the fifty bundles. I said good-bye to Bethany and Sarah, reminding them that I would see Bortheus and the other family and how I might be a bit late coming back. I walked from the house to the where the path meets the one to the tannery. Jehoiada and the others were just a few rods away and I turned to see Bethany and Sarah still standing in front of the house. I waved to them, and they waved back.

As we approached Joppa I said, "Good fortune, Jehoiada, the tax collectors aren't at their place."

"All it saves us, Father, is an argument, since they will carefully check the Luxor before it leaves and extract every penny from us. If they were here now, we would have to convince them this is to go aboard the Luxor. They know full well what is going on, but they try everything they can to collect twice, or even three times. I'm certain it will be difficult when we bring the second load later today."

When we got to the Luxor, the brothers and I waited with the carts while Jehoiada went aboard and checked the final loading arrangements. It was still early, but the level of activities was picking up all around us. This would be a busy day at the port of Joppa when the gentile shippers tried to make up for the Sabbath's quiet—an inconvenience to the captains and crews in this Jewish city.

When Jehoiada returned, I handed the bundles from the carts, and quickly the three others carried them two at a time up the gangplank. Jehoiada and the two brothers had broken into a sweat when another cart pulled up behind us and the driver shouted, "Hey, get that thing unloaded, and if you can't get it done in good time, move out of the way for some of us who can."

Angrily I turned to answer him in kind, then thought better of it and remained silent. It felt good to work hard, and we finished in less than half an hour.

Jehoiada and the brothers went back for the second load, and I decided to see Bortheus and meet them back at the Luxor in two hours. I watched them proceed down the street, then with my tool bag over one shoulder, Bortheus' sandals over the other, I started my journey. Past the waiting carts, up through the wakening market, I headed for my friend's house, but a long awaited encounter took precedence.

One stall was putting out fresh baked bread and sweet cakes. I smelled it before I saw it. The aroma caught me, carrying me momentarily back to the trip of so many years ago to the Jordan to see the Baptist. I bought sweet cakes for Bortheus and me, turned and stood face to face with Meraioth.

I was startled, so was he. I ran into the gathering crowds as he shouted, "Stop him! Get him!"

I ran as fast as I could back towards the ship, hoping to loose him in the loading and confusion there. And I would have lost him too, but for the strong, young guards with him.

As I turned a corner, a guard sent me sprawling across the road. As I started to get up, he hit me across the face and I gave up my futile resistance. A crowd quickly gathered around us, Meraioth pushed his way through and stood glaring in my face.

"So the great and mighty Malchus is a poor cobbler," he sneered in his offensive way that I suddenly remembered so well. "Perhaps your ailing master will take heart when he sees you. I do believe he had given you up for dead. And now, you will be dead."

Then to the guards he snapped, "Bind him and take him to the cell at the High Priest's palace. If he escapes, you will forfeit your lives."

They took no chances of my escape. The guards pulled my arms behind me and cinched the knots tight. The cords they used were from my own bag. They set me on a horse, tied my feet from under the horse, and just to make certain I couldn't get off, they tied another rope around my neck and secured it to the horse. If I fell, I realized, I would probably die.

With one guard in front and one behind, we left quickly for Jerusalem about a half days' journey away. At first, I was able to balance myself as the horse galloped, and even reflect on my predicament. Soon, however, the strength of the unused muscles in my back and legs was entirely spent and I was viciously jostled.

The pain was so excruciating that I continually screamed—silently, inside, so the guards would not hear me. I thought of the time I broke a tooth, and had it pulled. But this time I hurt like that everywhere.

My swollen hands were going numb. The intense pain in them began to subside, but I knew it would return with a vengeance when the cords were cut. The rest of my body hurt so badly I could not identify the specific places where the pain was registering. How long this lasted, I don't know, but it was more than I could bear. Mercifully, I lost consciousness.

When I awoke, I was on the ground, the two guards standing over me. They had cut the leather cords holding my hands. Blood was oozing from the place they cut into the flesh in order to cut the thongs. All the pain the numbness had suppressed now came rushing back. Guards or no guards, I screamed, and again fell into unconsciousness.

This time I awoke on the horse. My arms were tied at the elbows, and my feet at the ankles. I was draped over the horse on my stomach. Now my midsection hurt the most. The jostling, the pain, the heat and the dust in my face were too much. I vomited.

The spasms and retching continued long after every particle of food was expelled from my stomach. How long I lay like this, I don't know, but when again I became aware of my surroundings, I was free of the cords, lying on stones in a place of absolute darkness.

I painfully moved about in the dark, trying vainly to find a position of comfort. The cell was small, and if there was a way out, it had to be over my head. I suspected several ribs were broken, and one of my ankles was unable to bear any weight. When small amounts of light did begin to filter into my hovel, it was from far above.

My belly hurt so much that the thought of food was disgusting. But, I was desperately thirsty. My pain ridden body shook with chills and cramps. The thought of a drink of water caused my face to contort as if I were gulping down the precious liquid. I wept, but no tears came. I wept with pain and despair. l wept with loneliness and isolation. I wept for my family and friends. I wept for the misery and pain that surely awaited me. I wept for the agony of seeing Caiaphas. And, I wept because I was experiencing some of what Jesus experienced.

"Lord Jesus," I spoke to him who had promised to be with me, "thank you that you suffered all this and more for me. Thank you that even though you did not have to do it, you did it for me. Lord, I am so miserable, I'm in such agony, please come and help me. Please come and ease this pain and anguish. Prepare my heart, that I may serve you well in everything."

My prayers were interrupted as the large stone over the opening was moved away. The light hit my eyes like wind blown sand. I heard Meraioth's voice ordering the guards, "Get him out." A ladder was lowered into the cell, and a guard descended. He pushed and lifted, and somehow got me out of the pit.

Squinting my eyes, shaking my head, I identified the surroundings. I was in Caiaphas' courtyard near the place where I spent those years in his service. I was led, or rather, dragged upstairs to the living quarters, and pushed into the room where Caiaphas, now an old man, lay flat in a huge bed that accented the frailty of his worn-out body.

Meraioth spoke first. "My Lord Caiaphas, I have brought someone for you to see to give you some cheer and happiness in your time of illness."

Caiaphas opened his eyes and turned them towards Meraioth, but no other part of his body or his head moved. Meraioth continued, "I present to you this poor wretched cobbler named Malchus."

His eyes grew wide, and with obvious effort his head began to rise. He tried in vain to get an arm beneath him to rise up. He said, "Maal . . . Maa," and then began to cough the hacking cough of a dying man. His head fell back on the bed, and his hand made a flicking motion to get out. The guards immediately escorted me out.

As we left the room, Matthias entered. We continued down the stairs to the courtyard opening of the cell when Matthias called out "Meraioth, wait."

He quickly joined us and said, "Meraioth, I know you meant well, bringing this man here, but I do not want my father facing death with this unpleasantness. Come, we will draw up charges for the Romans and deliver him at once to the fortress." Then to the guards, "Give food and water and tend his wounds." I drank and ate too quickly. I could not keep the nourishment. I thought it would stay inside me, but when they washed me off to determine the extent of my injuries, I lost it. When they finished, I was able to drink water.

Soon Meraioth was back, his venomous eyes darting at me with hatred and contempt, "Even now the sweetness of my victory over you is turning sour," he said. "But your certain death at the hands of Rome is my vindication." Then to the guards, "Put him on a cart and take him to the fortress. Give this to the centurion in charge. Now go, get him out of here."

The brief trip to the Roman fortress ended too quickly. The cart had been my first place of meager respite since the arrest in Joppa. Two husky Roman soldiers took me to the centurion. Each one took an arm, I helped only a small amount. Romans were efficient in everything, including moving injured prisoners.

The centurion read aloud the charges. "Unfaithful and disobedient slave of Caiaphas, the servant and appointee of Caesar, former High Priest of Israel. This person is elusive and dangerous and has been a fugitive for many years. Now restored by the hand of God to his former master, we deliver him to Rome for justice and swift punishment. He is also a member of the sect known as Followers of the Way who subvert the Pax Romana by teaching that Jesus is Lord, not Caesar. Our recommendation is crucifixion. Signed, Matthias."

Looking at me he asked, "What is your name, slave that has so stirred up His Foolishness the High Priest?"

I almost said Simon, but my speech was slow and I corrected myself, "Malchus."

"Malchus. And what is your occupation Malchus?"

"I am a cobbler, sir. I make sandals," I answered.

He shook his head in mock agreement saying, "Oh yes, a most dangerous occupation. Well, we'd better be rid of you right away." He spoke to his soldiers, "Put this man in the common prison. Treat him well, and take him to Caesarea with the others tomorrow."

A ray of hope began to shine in me. Hope that would brighten or fade according to the whims of Roman soldiers.

CHAPTER TWENTY-FOUR

ROME

Now that the journeys of my remembrances are in prisons as well as the reality of my present situation, I feel no relief from the approaching dawn of Caesar's birthday. It is somewhere in the fourth watch of the night and Cleomus again joins me in my cell.

"Cleomus, I don't suppose I have any rights or authority in this, but my bag of tools that are somewhere here in the prison—anyway, I'd like you to have them. It's not much, but it's everything I own, all my earthly possessions. Can you get them and keep them?"

He answers "Yes, I can get them, and I'd like them very much. Thank you, Malchus."

I continue, "Also, Cleomus, I've wanted to ask you for a long time, but have been afraid, or concerned about your reaction. But now my desire is too strong to ignore. Can I pray for your arm? I see the pain you are in, and it would make me feel much better if I could pray for you."

He looks at me in a way I have never seen before, and nods his head. I gently place my hand on his upper arm right at the shoulder where I discern to be the source of the problem. He grimaces, even with the tender touch. I feel the disfigurement from the vicious sword blow. "Lord Jesus," I pray, "You are Lord of everything and you touched many people like my friend, Cleomus, and healed them. Thank you that you went through death for us and provided healing through your victory. In your name, Lord Jesus, I speak to the pain, 'stop afflicting

Cleomus.' I speak to the muscles and flesh, 'be renewed and made whole.' Thank you, Lord Jesus. So be it."

A tingling, hot sensation had flowed through my hand as well as a sensing of the rush of power. I look at Cleomus and just nod my head. He sits a moment longer just looking at me, and as usual of late, gets up and leaves without speaking. I am certain God touched him, and feel confident that if the healing is not instantaneous, it is at least started, and will be evident later.

JERUSALEM

Thinking of Cleomus' pain reminds me of my painful night in Jerusalem. Four of us prisoners shared the common cell at the Fortress Antonia, but that night is a blur in my memory. However, the trip to Caesarea is painfully clear. The four of us were chained together, and forced to walk. I was given a crutch to help, but the pain in my ankle was intense. The other three prisoners had no option but to help me because we were chained together.

The Romans were on horseback and cared little about our welfare. By noon of the first day we had traveled an unacceptably short distance, so the soldiers commandeered a cart that some poor farmer was driving. The four of us were put on the cart and we made better time.

I immediately fell into a deep and fitful sleep, tormented by the dreams of dying lambs and flashing swords. When I awoke, we had passed Joppa, and were on the road north to Caesarea. As dusk drew near, the soldiers allowed the farmer to return to his destination, many hours behind us, and we made camp for the night.

We, prisoners, had to rub down the horses together. Everything was done "together," as the chains kept us from separating for any reason. Then we prepared the only suitable ground for the Romans, who ate their fill of the provisions, while we ate the scraps of their meal. The soldiers slept in relative comfort, except the one who remained awake to watch us.

Our bedding consisted of rocky terrain, cold hard chains, and nothing else. It was a horrible night, filled with fitful flashes of sleep and the anxious awaiting of dawn. Had we known what dawn would bring, we would have relished the night.

Breakfast consisted of water and more scraps from the soldiers. I was surprisingly better in the morning, and with the help of the crutch, and of another prisoner. I managed to hobble along at the set pace. We pushed on from shortly after sun up, until past mid day. We finally collapsed, and the soldiers took a break.

There was bread for the soldiers, but no scraps for us. We drank our fill of water and lay on the ground while the soldiers laughed and made bets. At first we had no interest in their wagers, but to our horror found that we were the objects of their gambling. They were betting on who could run the longest before being dragged by the horses.

We were then separated from each other, but remained chained by a brutal cuff locked to our wrists. Each prisoner's chain was joined by a rope to the pommel of the saddle of a different horse. No one bet on me, so I brought up the rear, while the other three were run side by side. We started off at a trot. I was immediately dragged on the ground, but we soon stopped.

One prisoner refused to run, and an argument broke out among the soldiers. One of them wanted to scourge the resister, but another stopped him, saying, "No! My money is on him. If you scourge him, I lose and you win, If you scourge him, the bet is off."

The other soldier shot back, "Then you make him run, or you lose and pay up now."

Dismounting his horse the soldier approached the resister, still lying on the ground. He took him by the hair of his head and lifted him to his feet. The prisoner began to tremble. They stood in terrifying silence for a moment, then the wild-eyed, enraged soldier took the hand of the prisoner and with his teeth ripped off about half of one of his fingernails. The prisoner yelped with pain and grabbed the bleeding hand. The soldier took the injured finger in his hand, pulled it up to the space between their two faces and through clenched teeth barked, "Run! Win!"

I could not see the race since I was being dragged along the road at the end of the procession. They ran a long time before a prisoner dropped. I knew one of them had fallen because the soldiers either cheered or complained, and that horse dropped back next to the one pulling me. I looked at the miserable, sweat-drenched body being dragged next to me. It was not the original resister.

I was deposited in my cell at the prison in Caesarea which was built right in the sea wall of the Roman fortress. Many prisoners were held here awaiting transportation to Rome, and so an efficient prison existed. I knew none of this for several days. After being thrown into my isolated cell, I found a jug of water, which I greedily drained. There was no food, but the next time I awoke, there was food and a full jug of water.

For two or three days, I awoke only enough to eat and drink. I was vaguely aware of the passing of night and day, but little else registered in my tormented mind. As my health was slowly restored, I returned to the normal cycle of staying awake during the day, and sleeping at night; however, it was several weeks before I was able to walk without pain.

I remember well the day I realized that I felt healthy, or at least felt no excessive pain, and the gnawing feeling of hunger had ceased being unusual. Whether it was a feeling of health or the absence of pain didn't matter, it felt good. It came in my seventh month at Caesarea.

For the next six months I was swept into the routine of prison life at Caesarea. I learned to communicate with prisoners in nearby cells by tapping, always hoping that someone could take greetings from Malchus to the house of Simon the Tanner in Joppa. However, no one from this prison was set free during my tenure. Everyone went to Rome or to their death.

I knew nothing about my disposition. The only thing I ever heard was the official charges against me read by the centurion in Jerusalem. I didn't know if I was to be killed, tried or freed. After thirteen months, I thought I might live. I doubted I would be freed, although the mind is strong in its desire to be free.

Spring had come to the region. There were days when I felt the delicious warmth of the sun seeping into the wall of my cell. It was a good warmth this time of year, compared to the tortuous heat that transformed the cell into an oven, later in the summer. I was sitting against the wall, absorbing the heat, when I heard the footsteps of at least two guards. These footsteps, at this time of day, were not in the routine.

My heart raced as they fumbled with the door. Swinging the door wide open the first guard entered carrying my tool sack. He looked about the cell. The other one said, "Come with us. It's off to Rome for you."

Risking their anger, I asked as many questions as I dared. They only knew that I was going to Rome, and the ship was to sail with the tide.

The ship was a troop transport. A new detachment of soldiers was delivered to Caesarea, and a like number were returning to Rome. There were about thirty prisoners who shared an area at the bottom of the ship, behind the quarters for the soldiers.

The soldiers had bunks and a flat floor. We had sloping timbers and a wet floor. The trip could have been terrible, but to me, it was an exciting time. We were conscripted to labor on the ship, scrubbing and hauling and polishing. It was hard work, but a wonderful alternative to the days of inactivity in the cell.

Some of the soldiers also forced us to work for them, polishing or shining or doing whatever they desired. When it became known that I was a cobbler and my tool bag was on board, I spent the rest of the trip repairing and making sandals. I also spent the trip without the pangs of hunger, as grateful soldiers rewarded my efforts with food.

As I repaired their sandals, many asked why I was a prisoner. That gave me an opportunity to share about the Lord Jesus. I was not allowed to speak unless it was in answer to questions, so this became an exciting time. Several of the soldiers were seriously considering the message of Jesus' resurrection from the dead, and three of them promised me they would ask God to show them if this was true. This was as far as I was allowed to take them on their journey into the Kingdom of God.

This earthly journey to the city of Rome took only a few weeks. At the mouth of the Tiber river we, prisoners, were transferred to a barge so we would not detract from the triumphant entry of the soldiers into Rome.

We moved slowly up the Tiber as the first rays of the dawn streaked across the earth. We were heading northwest for a moment straight into the rising sun. Then the barge turned towards the east at the bottom of the famous "S" curve of the Tiber. I watched the Roman officer who stood by me. He appeared nearly overcome with emotion. Banners and symbols of mighty Rome abounded. Wherever our eyes looked, they soon found the Screaming Eagle.

Perhaps because I had made sandals for the officer, he took it upon himself to introduce me to the city. "See there to your right," he put a hand on my shoulder and pointed. "Those five flat-topped spurs are five of the seven hills of Rome. They are called the Aventine. And there, just ahead of those five is the Palatine Hill, and there, just over the bow of the barge is the Capitol Hill."

The rising sun struck the hills and caused them to stand out in relief from the rest of the city. They were seven patches of light in a sea of shadows. The officer was now so moved with emotion that he could barely speak. His face was flushed, and he finally stammered, "This is the mother of the kings of the earth."

Then turning to me, he spoke as I had heard other zealots speak, "You see, Caesar is not only the Ruler of the rulers of the earth, and the King over all kings, he is the Pontifex Maximus, the great bridge between the religious systems of all the gods, and man." Then, with proud eyes burning, he whispered boldly, "Caesar is Lord!"

A cold, prickly chill went down my spine. I said to myself, "Mother of kings? No! Mother of harlots!" Shivering with the ominous foreboding, I saw the dark, shadowed spaces between the seven hills as rivers running with the blood of the victims of "mother" Rome.

"Lord," I asked, "will my blood be a part of that river?"

CHAPTER TWENTY-FIVE

ROME

Dawn begins to lighten our cells, and a soft hymn of the victory of Jesus is beginning to lighten our souls as each prisoner quietly joins in the song. I am startled as Cleomus opens the door to my cell and says, "Demas is here, Malchus. Follow me."

We walk slowly past the cells of my brothers. I meet their eyes, and from some, the closed fist of victory. With a nod of my head and as much as possible, a look of encouragement, I return their gaze. I walk about a half step behind Cleomus and to his side. This part of my journey in life is with a gentile, and a Roman soldier who killed a brother just a few months ago, yet I find help and a feeling of friendship and yes, even brotherhood, with this man. I am glad that he is with me as we enter the room I've known before as an interrogation cell. Demas is waiting there. Demas seems out of place. His crisp, white tunic is cleaner and more presentable than any garments this prison has seen for some time. His beard is neatly trimmed, and every hair is in place. He rushes toward me saying, "Simon, Simon," then hesitates at my filth and odor. The embrace is now cautious and tentative, but I am glad he does embrace me.

"It is good to see you, Demas. I have been looking forward to seeing you, but worried about the nature of the visit. Let me just look at you for a moment," I say, examining him head to toe. "O Simon, Simon, what a pity; what a terrible thing to see you like this. You belong free, and in Joppa with Bethany and the church there. You don't belong in this place," he says with a sour look on his face. I'm not sure if his look of disdain is because of my predicament, or his own concern at being in this squalid prison.

"How is Paul, Demas? Is he well, and pressing on?" I ask.

A different expression crosses his face. I detect a note of superiority as Demas says, "Oh, I haven't seen brother Paul for some time. I am not traveling with him anymore. The work I am to do for God is centered in Thessalonica, and it is not right for me to be wandering all over the earth with him."

"What brings you to Rome, Demas?" I ask. "And how did you find out about me?"

"My father has a business in Thessalonica, and has been after me for some time to follow in his steps. It was clear to me that God wanted me to do that, and to witness to Christ from a position of success and wealth. Well," he continued, "the business requires that I make a trip to Rome once or twice a year. I saw John Mark, here in Rome, on my last trip, and the conversation included you. He said that Peter and the others were convinced that you were a prisoner here, although no one was certain. I asked about you, and had a little trouble until I used the name Malchus which John Mark was using. After visiting with the centurion in charge of the prisons, I gained permission to visit, and scheduled another business trip to bring me here."

"So, some of the brothers are aware that I'm here," I say.

"No, not really," Demas corrects. "I haven't seen any of the brothers since that time, and they were only surmising that you were here."

"Demas, have you stopped fellowshipping with the brothers, and the saints in Thessalonica?" I ask.

"My fellowship is with God, and with the others when it's right. But I am free, and not a slave to all those meetings and the legalistic structures that have been set up. It isn't at all like it was in Joppa," Demas continues. "There is no flow to the meetings, and I just don't get fed."

I feel the hot anger rising in my face, but before I express it, Demas continues, "Simon, we don't have much time, and I desperately want to help set you free from the misunderstandings that could cost you your life. You are not denying Jesus as the Christ by saying, 'Caesar is Lord!' You are just acknowledging that Caesar is Caesar."

"Simon, God wants you to be a fruitful witness of the life of Christ. Not just a witness, but a person experiencing the abundant life. Look at the promises of God; you are a child of Abraham. Paul said that all God's promises for Abraham belong to you. He did not call you to be poor, or sick, or weak. He called you to be blessed.

"Jesus came and took away all our sins, and all the reasons we can't do what God wants—but the responsibility is ours. It is man's. We are to rule over what God has made.

"God gave all this for us. We can solve problems—we can make things right. We can negotiate and persuade, and man will change. All will embrace the Christ and the Kingdom of God will come here to the earth in answer to our prayers.

"This tremendous nation—these buildings—the Senate—the Pax Romana—surely you don't think these happened without the blessing of God?

"All you have to do Simon is say, 'Caesar is Lord!' and then you can get back at the work of preaching and living."

I stand in stunned silence as Demas goes on, "What kind of a witness is this? If you're a free man, and wealthy and healthy, then others will envy you and be drawn to you. They will want what you have. Then, you can tell them about the Lord. You see, we need to build a bridge to the pagans on which it is easy to cross over into the Kingdom of God.

"What are you really saying when you say, 'Caesar is Lord!'? I heard Paul teach that there is no authority except that which comes from God, and we are to be submissive to the rulers—even Caesar. You can say Caesar is a ruler from God and therefore he is a lord. Even Christ said to give Caesar what is his, and this allegiance to Caesar is right and godly. You're not denying your faith at all in simply saying, 'Caesar is Lord!'

"Of course God is God. No one denies that. And Caesar is Caesar. He is the ruler of the mightiest empire on earth. He is a Lord.

"What would be the benefit of your death? God wants you to be happy with your wonderful wife and family. He instituted marriage. He did not institute killing people, or making them take oaths. Think of how much more you could do for God together with Bethany at your side, with her warmth and tenderness and understanding."

Cleomus steps between us and pushes Demas back with a force that causes him to stumble. Looking him hard in the eyes, he roars between clenched teeth, "Shut up, Demas! That's enough!" Demas' eyes grow wide and fear seems to engulf him from this outburst of rage from a Roman soldier.

Now Cleomus turns toward me and the anger slowly drains from his face. Cleomus asks, "All right, Malchus. What will it be? Are you going to say, 'Caesar is Lord!'? Or will you maintain your allegiance to the Lord Jesus Christ?"